The Island

H. Wakefield

A Wings ePress, Inc.
Mystery Novel

Wings ePress, Inc.

Edited by: Jeanne Smith
Copy Edited by: Christie Kraemer
Executive Editor: Jeanne Smith
Cover Artist: Trisha FitzGerald-Jung
Image: Pixabay

All rights reserved

Wings ePress Books
www.wingsepress.com

Published In the United States Of America

Wings ePress Inc.
3000 N. Rock Road
Newton, KS 67114

What They Are Saying About
The Island

“If this is as exciting as your first book, *The Boat*, hurry up and get me a copy.”

—John Hardy

“I couldn’t put the first book down. I want many more.”

—Lynn Finn

“I read both *The Boat* and *The Man in the Woods* and really enjoyed both. I am waiting for the next one. You truly have the gift of story-telling.”

—Wilma Jackson

Dedication

To my family, friends and others who inspired me along
this journey while encouraging me
to keep writing and storytelling.

* * *

One

Life is not easy; it never was, nor will it ever be...get used to it. There are only two kinds of people: the quick or the dead. I was certainly hoping and praying with all my heart and soul that would not be my last thought as I exited this world.

I'm crouched here on the floor with my dogs in a wretched shack while being shot at in the dark of night. Who is firing the gun? Why? I don't know anyone on this damn rock of an island in the middle of nowhere off the Maine coast. I am acutely aware I am alone and out-gunned. Even though I have a gun, it would be no match for the high-powered rifle they're using. I'm certain they also have night vision. I know the natives here hate outsiders, but this is truly overkill.

My mind is running backwards at warp speed trying to make some sense of anything. Other than the two facts...I'm alone and trapped, I have nothing of any relevance surfacing.

Let me take you on the journey and show you how I got myself into this mess. First, I want to let you know I was an energetic and thankfully not easily frightened older woman who, for the most of her life, had lived solo and enjoyed the freedom that lifestyle provided: my three children grown, independent, with lives of their own. However, as a cautionary, there are limits for everything.

I'd reached my max capacity to deal with any and everything going on, not just in my life, but for those around me. I'd always thought I was a caring and helpful person to everyone. Now I found myself completely, thoroughly, and absolutely tapped out...big time. I am shockingly aware there is nothing of any value left to offer either for myself or anyone else.

Too much sickness, too many deaths...too many friends lost, either through death, moving, and/or life circumstance. I was bereft and feeling very alone and isolated. Never a good place for me. I'd always lived an isolated life, by choice. I needed to change the situation, now.

Once I realized that fact, it was time to do something. An older person I'd dearly loved, and trusted their wisdom once told me to not stand still. Do something, even though it was wrong. Inertia and stagnation were killers of the soul, mind, and body. I always believed that to be true to the very base of my being.

I would take my camper for a romp. It is ancient, but still very comfortable for me and my little dog, Miss Joy. I needed to pack up and go on an extended trip, because my world and I personally, were on the verge of exploding or imploding. A geographical change would be curative for both of us.

I headed to our local Walmart to get supplies for the camper. As I pulled into the parking lot, I saw a person at the very outer edge of the lot with a couple of dogs. This in itself would not have seemed unusual. Lots of folks rest and walk their dogs there.

However, the person was severely beating one of the dogs. As I got closer, I could see it was a creepy looking guy with long dirty hair and filthy clothing. He wasn't just correcting the animal...he was beating the dog with his fists and kicking and stomping its body. Sorry, that won't work in my world. I turned my truck into his space and got out. He was either high on drugs or just a freaking nutcase. He was on the verge of beating this Rotti almost to death, and she wasn't doing anything to deserve it. She was absolutely covered with blood on her head and chest. The only thing keeping her upright at all was the death grip he had on her collar.

There were two other dogs tied to the back of his trashy truck. They looked like pit crosses and were large males, from what I could see. They were cowering and had backed away as far as their ropes would allow them. They looked terrified. I jumped out of my truck and hollered as loudly as possible, "What in the devil are you doing to this animal?"

His response, "Mind your own damn business, bitch."

Wrong answer to me!

I was appalled at what he had already done to the animal. "Stop right now, or I'll call the police!"

"Screw you and the cow you rode in on. It's my damned dog, and if I want to beat her to death, that's my business and none of yours, so get lost before I give you some of the same." With that, he began to punch her again in the head.

I was done. I stepped up and told him, "If you're this angry, then hit me, but leave her alone."

Sometimes I'm not sure if a rational person lives inside of me. My mouth runs faster than my alleged brain. He towered over my five-foot-one-inch frame by at least a foot and outweighed me by over a hundred pounds. He threw his fist back as if to punch me, then appeared to think better of it. He snarled, "I got this bitch to breed with my males and all she wants to do is show her teeth and growl at them. If you're so damned interested in her, then take her." He passed me her rope he had tied to his truck. I took it and pulled her to me.

She understood at once I had saved her from any more abuse. His next statement almost floored me. "I paid a lot of money for her and I expect to be paid if you're going to take her." He yelled after me, "I got her for breeding and she ain't worth shit."

I asked her sit, and was trying to figure out my options when I noticed the tattoo on her stomach. My reply was easy, "If you paid a lot of money for a dog to breed, you aren't very smart...she's a spayed female." I didn't add that she was only pet quality, if that. I could see by the expression on his face he had no earthly idea what I was telling him. Stupid is still stupid. I also knew I couldn't afford an outlay of much money. I was dealing with too many other issues of my own to take on any more problems and/or expenses.

"What the hell are you talking about, you dumb broad?"

I told him to come forward and look at the tattoo. I stood by the dog's head and showed him the marking on her belly. "You mean that shows she can't have puppies?"

My answer was just short of a sneer. "Yep, for sure, that's how the vet marks his work when he does the surgery."

"Well, I still want some money for her."

"I don't have any money. The one thing I will do is call the Animal Control Officer and have her removed from your care right now. I'll also press animal cruelty charges against you."

I walked her to my truck, took out a bottle of water and paper towels and began to clean her up. He had broken one of her teeth and her eye was almost swollen shut. She was limping on her front leg. He had stomped her so hard on that paw it looked like her toe was almost ripped off. I would take her to my vet at once. At the very least, I could keep her safe from this idiot. I didn't care; she was in my care now and I would never give her back to that moron.

"Just take the bitch and get out of my sight."

"I need something in writing stating you gave her to me so I can get her treated and registered." As I was saying this, I was grabbing a pad of paper and pencil out of the boot in my truck door. I began writing.

"All right, I gave you the damned dog. Where do I sign?" I wrote, he signed, and she was mine. I drove away. I named her Mercy, right then and there. She certainly needed some mercy.

Two

While I was waiting at the vet's office, I talked to a person in the waiting room. He was laughing and telling me about an ad he had seen in one of the magazines about a rustic cottage on an island out in the ocean. It seemed it was only accessible by water taxi. The taxi came two days a week. He said the rental amount was dirt cheap because there wasn't any indoor plumbing, and it was on a remote part of the island, so you had to carry in all your supplies over a footpath. His parting sentiment as he went into the exam room was that only an idiot would ever rent anything like that.

This 'idiot' began rooting around trying to find the ad he mentioned. To be honest, the cabin sounded like paradise to me. After a short search, I found the advertisement he had been speaking about. I hate to admit this, but I tore it out of the publication because at the exact moment I found it, they called my name.

When my vet saw Mercy, he looked at me with a very stern expression on his face. His first words were, "Tell me this dog was hit by a car, truck, or a train. This isn't your dog, is it?"

I nodded along with my reply. "She is now. No, I didn't do this to her, and she did not get hit by anything but a depraved human." I went on to explain how I happened upon the scene in the parking lot and my having the dog being the end result.

Mercy's injuries would heal, the vet assured me, with time and good care. She had no broken bones other than the toe he had explained needed to be removed at once. The tooth would not be an overall problem to her eating or digestion. He cautioned me it might take weeks or longer for all of bruises to heal. He was mostly concerned about how she would react emotionally to the trauma. I wasn't concerned. I had owned a Rottie years ago and she was as gentle as a lamb. However, she had never been abused. I was sure the fact Miss Joy and I lived a pretty solitary and quiet life would be an asset to her healing, both physically and mentally.

In the past, I'd rescued other abused dogs and they had always been grateful and some of the best pets I'd ever owned. Owned is the wrong word here...they allowed me to enjoy their living with me.

When I brought her home with me, and my little old dog met her, it was touching. I don't begin to know how dogs communicate with each other, but Miss Joy instantly knew something was terribly wrong with Mercy and understood she was in pain. Mercy walked to the rug beside my rocker and carefully laid down. Miss Joy walked over, sniffed her, then began to lick her poor injured face. A few minutes later, Miss Joy went to her toy box, carefully selected a stuffed animal, brought it over and placed it gently on Mercy's paw.

Miss Joy is a miniature Australian shepherd weighing about eighteen pounds and is now going gray on her muzzle. She still loves to walk and play, but is slowing down, much like me. She is in her late teens and I'm in my late seventies.

Three

Mercy had only been with us for a couple of days when I decided to take the two of them for a walk on one of the local trails we frequented. It is a public trail by the river and never too crowded. It was late afternoon and still warm enough to not need a sweater or jacket. I hadn't walked Mercy before, other than to take her into the vet's office.

I had Miss Joy on her retractable leash and I snapped my shorter, heavier leash on Mercy's new collar. I soon found she would walk very comfortably close beside me, unlike Miss Joy who is always out at the very end of her leash and pulling me for all she is worth. I was praying perhaps she would learn proper etiquette from Mercy's example.

We had completed our loop and were returning to the truck when I noticed something wasn't right by the vehicle. From where I stood, I could see what appeared to be legs by the far side of my truck, facing the direction of the passenger side. Something was amiss. I pulled Miss Joy back toward me and very quietly rounded the back of my truck where I found a man reaching across the floor to where my purse was stashed under the driver's seat. I was incensed. How dare someone break into my vehicle and attempt to seal my property?

Without ever thinking about it, just as he was pulling himself out with my purse in his hand and a flat bar in the other, he began to straighten up as I grabbed the leash that was attached loosely to Miss Joy, wrapped it firmly around his neck and pulled it tight. He wasn't a large male, but he was shocked for the moment. He dropped my purse on the floor and grabbed for the cord around his neck. "What the hell are you doing? You're choking me."

My reply? "You're robbing me."

The scrap was on, but only for a moment. Mercy immediately understood I was in danger. She blocked up and began to snarl with her lips rolled back, showing her teeth.

"Call off that damn dog or she'll kill me," were the only words he could choke out. I had forgotten I was still tightening the leash around his neck. I called 911 on my cell, which thankfully I had in my pocket.

When the police arrived, they took one look at the dude and uttered, "Well Slim, I see you didn't learn anything from the last time."

He turned to me. "You can unleash him, lady. It isn't safe to leave your car anywhere anymore. If he wasn't so damn lazy, he'd jack it up and steal your wheels and tires."

Four

The first thing I did when I returned home was call the number on the ad for the remote cabin. A lady answered, and I tried to explain my interest. She muttered something then yelled to someone. "Bud, it's another call about that stupid shack." There was the sound of the instrument being dropped. I could hear conversation in the background but couldn't make out the words. I waited.

A querulous man's voice finally came on the line. "If this is another prank call, don't waste my time. The camp is what it is and nothing more than described in the ad. It ain't fancy and that's not going to change. And no, I am not going to rent it for less because of the conditions. Now, what in hell do you want to know?"

His answer took me aback, but I was determined to at least get some more information. "I need to know if you allow dogs? I understand there isn't any electricity, so how do you keep food from spoiling? What is the rental period you are advertising for?"

When he began to speak, I knew he was over his concern about it being another crank call. "It's a shack. Why would I care if you brought a dog with you? I don't care how many of you come, either; the rent stays the same. There's an old spring box behind the camp and you can keep stuff cold in there if you put it in plastic bags. There is an outhouse, and you can walk through the woods to the shore to wash. I left an old wooden punt on the shore with the oars under it. You can use that, but it leaks some, so you have to bail. You need to carry any supplies from the far end of the island. There's a trail you can follow. When were you looking to rent, and for how long? I get paid in advance. There are very few telephones on the island and the natives are not friendly because they don't want me to rent to strangers. I'm just letting you know ahead of time. There are also no stores on that rock, so either you haul it in or go without. That includes toilet paper. Do I make myself clear?"

To say it was not a 'friendly' call was crystal clear. "I understand your position clearly. How soon is the camp available? How does anyone find you to make arrangements and would I need to schedule the water taxi through you?"

His reply was instant. "I can meet you wherever you want and I will give you the number for the water taxi. Once I have your money for my rent, you are on your own, period. Do you understand that?"

"I do understand what you are saying, but what if there is an issue with something out there? Who do I contact?"

He became very gruff, "Did you listen to anything I just explained to you? It is what it is...the camp is not part of the Hilton chain. There isn't any running water, sewerage, electricity, maid service and no key. You take what you want out there and that is all there is. I don't supply anything, so there is nothing to go wrong or mess up. If you were going to pitch a tent in the middle of the damn woods, it's the same damn thing, only in this case there is a shack there. Either you are interested or not; just don't bother me anymore. I also want cash."

I expected to hear the line go dead. In my mind, I was trying to decide if at my age and ability I wanted to, or if I could, carry in enough supplies for the dogs and myself to keep us for a week or so until the taxi would come back. I ventured it wouldn't be the first or the last foolish thing I would ever do. "I would like to rent it for a week with the option to extend, it if that works for you. When would it be available?"

We made our deal, met up to give him the funds, and got the number for the water taxi. I was surprised when I met him, as I had pictured him in my mind to be an older man. He was in his late forties, a middle-sized person, and as far as I could ascertain, almost totally void of personality. He didn't introduce himself, nor was he interested in who I was. Finally, he grudgingly gave me his name: Dan Cleaves. I gave him the rent for the week, and he gave me the number for the water taxi.

He finally said, "If you want more than the week, call me, and give the boat captain the cash to pay me when he gets back to the dock."

I had reservations about the whole thing, but figured what the deuce? I needed a change, and I could always write it off to being stupid. I went home to pack. I have a large LL Bean pack basket, a bedroll, a large duffel, and a collapsible spinning rod. I packed a minimal amount of clothes, dog treats, and enough light food for me. With the pack basket and two bags, I was sure we would survive. I grew up on an island, so I wasn't concerned about starving. The one thing I did pack was my trusty Colt Detective Special 38. When I travel, I never leave home without it or a supply of bullets.

I met the water taxi down at the public pier on Jellerson Harbor. He not only serviced some of the offshore islands for passengers, he also delivered mail. I liked Captain Tom at once. He was an older man not quite my age, but close. We chatted while he waited for a couple more folks to arrive. He was not concerned about my dogs. He was surprised I was going alone to the 'shack,' as he referred to it. He explained nicely if I wanted more supplies brought over, I needed to call the store on the mainland, and order them and he would pick them up on his way to the boat. I took the card with the numbers on it and carefully tucked it into my pocket.

The ride to the island was longer than I expected, but very pleasant. I loved being on the water again. He told me he was sorry he couldn't land me closer to my part of the island, but there wasn't any dockage and it was too rocky to risk it. He off-loaded some supplies and the mail to a man he called Mr. Peasly, who arrived with a small lawn tractor/mower and a little trailer. When Captain Tom tried to introduce him to me, the man just shook his head and walked away with his supplies. Welcome or basic manners were definitely not his strong suit. Captain Tom looked at me and asked, "Are you certain you want to stay here? I can take you back now."

I smiled and told him I'd be fine. Loaded up my gear, gathered the dog leashes, and we set off for the hike to begin our new adventure.

Five

The 'cabin' was a shack. The small porch was ready to fall off and was hardly able to hold my weight. The door was half open and had been that way for a while. There was a pile of leaves in the middle of the room, and others blown as far as the wind could carry them. It was just one open room with a wood stove in the center and a makeshift counter that consisted of a board braced up for what I assumed would be considered the kitchen. I found an old cast iron fry pan, a pot that looked like it was older than I was, a ratty coffee pot, and some utensils I was certain had been left by Columbus.

I saw what looked like a handmade box with legs for a bed. It had a piece of canvas nailed over the frame. I had to smile...at least there wasn't any issue with bed bugs.

I found the remnants of a broom and set about getting the debris out of the camp. Knowing the nights would be chilly, I looked around outside for wood. I found a few pieces, but it was clear I was on my own if I wanted warmth. I did find an old hatchet with a handle that had been taped to keep it together. Hanging on the side of the building was an ancient buck saw. I was good. In days gone by, I had gathered wood to heat an entire house in the middle of the winter in Downeast Maine.

I checked out the outhouse. It looked ready to fall over in a strong wind. It wasn't the worst one I had ever encountered.

Once I got our stuff unpacked and the food in the spring to keep it cool, it was still light enough to explore a bit. I wasn't upset about the camp. It was certainly primitive for sure, but I didn't care. For once, I was not looking to purchase it.

The dogs and I walked down the foot path to the ocean. It not only smelled good in the pine woods—a special treat was the fact the stand of woods hadn't been touched in forever. There were some of the largest, tall, straight trees I had seen in a very long time, the advantage to being way offshore and not worth the cost of harvesting the wood. What a blessing. The sunshine was slanting through and throwing a soft light, which reminded me of light coming through stained glass windows in an old church. I could hear the birds singing as I walked along on the mosey trail. The dogs were walking together close to me. Life seldom ever gets that good.

We walked out of the woods to the shoreline. What a photo op! The shore was rocky with a small cove cut into the center of the rocks. A small perfectly crescent-shaped white sand beach was there.

We found the punt where Dan had said it would be. The oars were under it. When I tried to pick it up to flip it over, I thought it would fall apart. It was not in great shape, period. I was more concerned it would fall apart rather than how much it would leak.

I laughed at the dogs. Usually if Miss Joy is loose, she is exploring, but always within sight of me. Today, Mercy was sitting close to me, and Miss Joy was sitting in front of her forelegs, and leaning back as if for support. Thank God they can't talk, or they would have been saying, 'What has this crazy woman gotten us into now?'

We walked out on the rocks so I could see how deep the water was and to determine if there was any chance there would be any fish this close to shore. As I was coming back across the rocks, I noticed there was a place where perhaps I could harvest some mussels and, with luck, at low tide dig some clams. Yes, I was going to enjoy being there. Tomorrow, I would explore some more and see if I could find berries to eat.

As we walked back to the cabin, I could hear the squirrels chattering away up in the trees. Life was getting good again.

I had brought a folding plastic bottle with me, so we filled it with the water from the spring and began to start a fire so we could fix ourselves some food. I was tired from the day's activities and it would soon be dark. I wanted to be rested for tomorrow. I planned to use and enjoy every moment of this time to the fullest. With that thought in mind, and Miss Joy curled up next to my tummy with Mercy stretched out the entire length of my back, I fell asleep.

When daylight filled the camp, I was startled, because for the first time in forever, I had slept all night and had not endured one nightmare. What a blessing!

We made our way outside to do our morning business, then I went about making a small fire for morning coffee and dog feeding. I had brought along a bag of regular coffee because I don't like instant, and the weight was about the same. I had instant oatmeal and coffee while the girls crunched up their kibble. I had no idea what time it was and didn't care enough to check my cell phone. For this trip, we would be on 'our' time.

The day promised to be warm and sunny, so it seemed like a good time to check out the boat and fishing. I grabbed the small rod, a handful of dog bones and a cheese snack for me. I filled my canteen at the spring and checked to make certain nothing had bothered our food supply stashed there. We were off to the shore to play. I felt like an island kid again.

The tide was in, so I didn't have too far to haul the boat to get it into the water. For as old and decrepit as the punt was, it was a heavy haul to the water. Someone had left an old bleach bottle they had cut to make a scoop for bailing. I made sure we had that. The boat was pretty well dried out, so I knew I would do a lot of water removal. I just had to hope I was a more productive bailer than the boat was a leaker, or a bottom board would not just fall off and sink us altogether.

I had always taken Miss Joy in my kayak, so I knew she would be okay. When I asked Mercy to get in, she just stared at me with that 'what in the devil are you wanting' look. The deck was already showing signs of leaking, so I stepped into the boat to scoop out a bit of water. As soon as I stood in the boat and began to bail, Mercy made a massive leap, landing at my feet. I nearly lost my balance because I never saw her coming. Miss Joy was sitting on the prow seat. I wanted to see what Mercy would do, so I sat on the middle seat so I could row. Mercy stood for a few moments then moved to the back seat and sat on it. I guessed we had all figured out our places, so I put the oar locks up and slid the oars into them. The cove was calm and not deep, so if Mercy decided to abandon ship, she would be all right. Thankfully, dogs come with swim lessons installed in their brains and no YMCA training required.

I rowed around in a small circle, watching the dogs. They were fine. Now on the other hand, rowing that big old barge of a wooden punt was a far cry from paddling my fiberglass kayak. We were definitely not going to row to the mainland anytime soon.

Once I got outside of the cove, I baited my hook, just like I had millions of times before when I was a kid on the island putting it overboard. Within minutes, I had a bite and my excitement soared. It had been a very long time since I'd fished. I had a sudden concern; what would either of the dogs do when I hauled a flopping fish into the boat? Too late now. I was already reeling it in. I couldn't believe my eyes...a mackerel! My very favorite fish. It flopped on the deck while Mercy kept watch and Miss Joy didn't seem to care. We were good!

When I returned to shore, the tide was not as high but it was manageable to get the punt up onto the sand far enough so I could moor it with a rock tied to the prow line. I found a nice bed of mussels and harvested some for my dinner. I fried up my fish and steamed my mussels in foil and enjoyed it all with a nice cup of merlot. We sat outside on the edge of the decaying deck enjoying the sunset. I was happy. The dogs were content, and I didn't even care about the state of the deck and was pleased that, for once, it wasn't mine to repair.

That day seemed to set the pattern for our next couple of days. We explored our end of the island along the shore, played in the boat, fished, gathered mussels and clams to eat and relax.

On our second day, while exploring the island, we encountered two men on the pathway. They appeared shocked to see anyone there. To be truthful, so was I. I smiled and called the dogs to me. They turned abruptly without a word, and walked back the way they had come. I wasn't surprised, considering the snub from the day we arrived. I never gave it another thought. We finished our walk and returned to the cabin. We would spend time out in the boat and do some fishing. I would never tire of eating fresh seafood.

We walked down to the shore and hauled the boat to the water. I always had a chuckle while I was doing this, because no matter what time of day I decided to launch the boat, the water was always out further than the boat, requiring me to drag it. It was a fun exercise.

As I was pulling the boat down to the waterline, I noticed a small skiff up in the cove. It wasn't any of my business. I was sure the natives fished here just as I was doing. When the person in the skiff spotted me, he immediately gunned his motor and left the cove. Ah, more fish for me. We rowed and fished the afternoon away. What a pleasant time out in the sun. By the time we returned to the shore, we were all comfortable in that lazy sort of way that just restores your senses.

I began to regain some semblance of order to my thinking regarding enjoying the simple things in my life. The dogs were great companions, always ready to join me, or to just sit quietly and watch the sun rise or set.

<h1 align="center">*Six*</h1>

On the third day of our adventure, when we returned to the shack from our walk, I found the place had been tossed. Literally. Our stuff was thrown all over the room, and a note was scrawled on my pad of paper. It read, "GET THE HELL OUT OF HERE NOW!" I knew this was not the action of kids playing a prank on outsiders. I was raised on an island, and as kids, we were somewhat naughty but never malicious.

I knew the island people didn't like outsiders here, but I didn't ever feel they would be vicious about it. I contemplated what to do next as I rearranged our things. I was happy in the secret part of my heart, because I had been carrying my revolver with me. I would always keep it with me now. I was uneasy, but didn't feel really threatened.

I decided to go fishing and play with the boat for a bit. We walked down to the shore and got the punt into the water for a little row before fishing, just to explore further up in the cove. We had been on the water for probably an hour, and I was rowing back to our cove to begin fishing for dinner when I heard a power boat. It was odd, because as long as we had been at the shack, no large boats had been in our area. I had heard the lobster boats on the open water, but this one was really close and moving rapidly. I rowed toward the shore to be out of the way of the wake.

The boat was coming full blast straight for us when, at the last moment, it veered away, creating a large roll of wake to rock our small boat. We were all okay, but I was wondering what on earth that was all about. He made a circle and was coming straight back at us again. I rowed and hoped he would run aground on the rocks just under the water at the edge of the jetty. Those rocks formed the outside edge of our cove. Instead, he slowed and shouted over a megaphone, "Get the hell out or else." With that, he gunned the engines and powered out toward the open water.

I didn't get the name or the numbers off the boat because I was too busy trying to make sure we were safe. The incident shook me to the core. How could our being there be so distressing to anyone? I pulled the boat out of the water and tied it to the rock. I gathered some mussels for dinner and we walked back to the shack. No one had messed with it since we left it earlier.

When we sat out on the deck later that afternoon, I was not confident we were not being watched. The dogs were restless, but I wasn't certain they were not picking up on my discomfort. So much for peace and communing with nature.

We had a restless night, as I spent most of it listening for strange sounds. I slept with the revolver under my pillow. I knew there wasn't any point in walking into the village or whatever was considered the center of this hatred-centered place. There would be no assistance available to an outsider.

The morning dawned with a gloomy layer of fog. I hoped it would clear when the sun rose higher in the sky. We ate breakfast and watched as the fog began to lift. By my second cup of coffee, I was more hopeful it would be a better day than yesterday. We walked down to the cove, and I was shocked to see the punt smashed to pieces. In the sand next to the pile of debris was written in large letters, "GET OUT." I knew I had to do something, because it was apparent we were no longer safe on the island.

The water taxi would come on the next day, so that meant we would have to spend another night at the shack. I went into the room and began to mentally pack everything we would not need for the rest of our stay. My heart was saddened. Our adventure had turned into a nightmare. But why?

I was certain everyone knew the soonest I could vacate the premises was tomorrow because there was no other way to get off the island. I kind of hoped, because of this, we wouldn't be harassed today. I was wrong.

Seven

We were down on the shore walking on the rocks and just passing time when I spotted a man standing on the rock jetty by our cove. He was watching us. I couldn't make out his age from that distance. He was a tall man, and though he was not thin, he wasn't a heavily built man. I turned the dogs in that direction and when Mercy saw the stranger, she blocked up and stayed right by my side with Miss Joy next to her.

As we drew nearer, he walked in toward the edge of the path. I could now see well enough to know he was not a young man, but was perhaps a little younger than I. His hair was white and he had blue eyes and a dark tan, leading me to believe he was an outdoors person. He had a badge I couldn't identify attached to his belt. He was also carrying a small automatic handgun in a holster. Interesting, he wasn't wearing a uniform, but was certainly some form of law enforcement.

He didn't make any move toward us as I kept walking. Finally, he spoke, "I'm officer Gary Cole with the sheriff's office. I need to speak with you. What is your name, and why are you here?"

"Well, you've saved me a trip to find someone. I'm Kate Larson. I rented this cabin for a week and, as you can see, vandals trashed the boat last night and left their message in the sand. Yesterday, they tore up the cabin and left me a note to get out. Later in the day, a boat came into the cove and tried to ram us while we were in the punt and hollered a message for us to get out. Who called you?"

"Nobody *called* me. I'm here on official business. Where were you yesterday afternoon and last night?"

I was perplexed. "We were right here in this area. I just told you we came back to find the cabin tossed, then we nearly got rammed by a boat in the cove. What is your 'official' business, if I may ask?"

As I watched his face, he seemed to be having an internal debate, and it took him a few moments to answer. "I'm investigating a murder. Do you have any witnesses to where you were and what times you were there?"

I was flabbergasted, to say the least. I'd been threatened, harassed, my belongings trashed and then asked for proof of where I was. "Witnesses for what? I rented this shack for me and my dogs to have some peace and quiet. We are here alone, and other than the very unfriendly Mr. Peasly, who totally disregarded us when we arrived on the water taxi with Captain Tom, I have only seen the two men I met on the path yesterday before noon. I didn't speak to them and they had nothing to say to me. When we met them, they turned and hurriedly walked back in the direction they came from.

"Later the same day, we saw a person in the upper end of the cove in a metal skiff. Again, we never met or spoke. I have not spoken to anyone on the island, nor do I care to.

"The person who was running the power boat yesterday I couldn't identify if I fell over him, because he was too far away and he was wearing a strange hat that flopped down over his head. Also, the boat was not the average lobster boat usually found around here. Unfortunately, I didn't get the name or numbers, if it had any, because I was too busy trying to keep us safe."

I had a second thought, "Why would you come way out here to see me if you're investigating a murder? That seems strange, as I don't know anyone here and they don't know me nor do they want to. Are you talking about a crime here on the island or on the mainland?"

Again, he looked like he was pondering the question. At first, I thought it was pretty straightforward...apparently not. When he spoke, he seemed hesitant. "This is a crime that was committed here on the island. I arrived from the mainland to investigate it. How long have you been here? Why did you come to such a deserted place? Why are you here alone? How long were you planning on staying?"

Well, once he got himself into gear, he seemed to have a bevy of questions. "I've been here four days. I rented the camp for a week, but with all the vandalism and apparent hatred for strangers, I was going to leave tomorrow when the water taxi arrived. I rented the place to escape a bunch of craziness, which somehow seems to have infected every inch of the globe. I might add it seems to have extended to include this place as well. I came alone because I *am* alone and have been for many years. Is vacationing alone a crime now?"

Unbidden by him, I was certain, he almost smiled but not before the humor showed in his eyes. He tried to recover his 'official cop' voice before speaking. He said, "How anyone vacations, isn't a crime I'm aware of. However, you seem to be the only stranger on the island. Sorry to say, it lends itself to discussion, as there has never been a murder on this island as long as the residents can recall. Is your big dog always with you? Where have you traveled while you've been here and when?"

Easy answer for me. "My dogs are always with me. Both of them. I can show you easily where we have been since we came. Why are you asking about Mercy?"

Again, he had resumed his guarded look. He finally managed to speak. "There was a large dog at the scene of the crime and the first person to speak with me told me you had a killer dog with you. He thought it was a pit bull. He has his breeds mixed up for certain. How old is she? She seems very attached to you. How long have you had her?"

My explanation was short and sweet. "I haven't had her long... she's a dog I rescued from an idiot who was trying to beat and kick her to death because she wouldn't breed with his male pit bulls. He was almost as stupid as whoever told you I had a killer dog. First of all, she is a spayed female. Do you wonder why she wouldn't be interested in breeding? The vet checked her out and besides a broken tooth and a toe which had to be amputated and some facial stitches, she's fine. One of the humorous aspects of her trauma was when the vet stitched the injury to her face, the laceration was so extensive it required lots of suturing. The procedure left her with a slight pucker in the skin over her eye so she appears to have a perpetually quizzical look on her face. Things like that were the reason I came out to this God forsaken place for a chance to reclaim some sense of normalcy. It obviously didn't work."

Officer Gary seemed taken aback by my dissertation on the state of the world and the idiots in it. He stood pondering, then asked, "Would you show me where they amputated her toe?"

Now it was my turn to gape. What an odd request. "Of course, I can show you. I don't think there is any issue with your coming near us as long as it is not in a menacing manner."

As Gary approached, Mercy sat quietly at my feet while Miss Joy seemed more concerned. I reached down and lifted her front foot so he could clearly see there was no toe there. He reached out his hand with the palm up and spoke softly to her, "It's okay, girl, I would never hurt you or your little buddy here." He gave each of the dogs a pat then stepped back.

He turned his attention to me and asked another odd question. "What size shoe do you wear and how many pairs did you bring with you? How much do you weigh?"

If his manner had been more assertive or aggressive, I would have been offended, but they seemed like fair questions, so I responded. "I wear an eight and a half shoe, I have the ones I have on and a pair of old sneakers for walking in the water with me. I weigh about one hundred and thirty-five pounds. What you see is what there is to us. Any more questions?"

Gary grinned. "Nope, that was all I needed to know. Do you feel safe staying here until the boat comes tomorrow afternoon?"

"No, I don't, but it is the only place we can stay. I will tell you this, and, for obvious reasons, I don't want it to go any further. I have a .38

revolver with me and I have a permit to carry. If someone threatens me or the dogs, I would use it for protection."

He looked slightly taken aback but not overly shocked. "Would you use it? It does make me feel more comfortable about your being here alone with nothing. Do you have a cell phone with you, and do you have any service on this part of the island?"

"I have a cell, and no, the service is sketchy here, so I don't rely on it. I'm almost positive if you told anyone you were coming out here, we have an audience, even though they are out of sight. The dogs were restless even before you arrived. I don't envy you your job dealing with these folks. Do you have any idea what is going on that ended in this mess, or is it too early to get a handle on the issue?"

At first, I thought he wasn't going to answer, then, "I'm truly not sure what led up to the crime or who all is involved. I can tell you this: it was plain and simply a murder. Now I have to find out the who, what and why of the whole thing. I'm going to start back to the village. I understand what you said about not having another place to stay...I'm here on official business, and the folks that live here don't want me here either. Here is my card with my cell number. I don't have any better reception than you do, but if something happens, try to call me, please. If I don't hear from you, I will look for you and the dogs at the landing tomorrow afternoon to make certain you are away from here. Good luck, and for God's sake, be vigilant. Take care now."

As Gary walked away, I had a feeling we would be seeing him again.

Eight

We ate our lunch, then went to the shore to see if we could find my fishing rod I'd left in the boat before they trashed it. Perhaps with luck and the coming tide, I could catch one last fish for dinner to end our stay on a modestly high note. I was so bummed because something which could have been so good for us had turned so sour. It seemed the whole world was nuts.

We did find the rod in one piece and walked out on the jetty to see if we could snag dinner. Our luck held, and I caught two tinker mackerel. We would have one last nice meal, then I would finish packing our stuff.

I knew we most likely would not get through the night without some problem, so I had on my sweats, with my shoes by the bed for easy access. We had just settled down for the night when Mercy began to growl...a low rumbling sound I hadn't heard from her before. Miss Joy pressed closer to me but didn't make a sound. I wasn't sure what was going on outside, but didn't want to take any chances, so I took the revolver and rolled off the bed onto the floor while holding Miss Joy to me. Mercy slowly climbed down and tucked in next to me. We waited and listened. Suddenly, the window on the backside of the camp exploded. I knew it wasn't from a thrown rock because the blast shattered a part of the cabin door. Someone had a high-powered rifle with a silencer on it.

I knew we needed to get out of there and fast. I assumed if they had that kind of equipment, they also had night vision glasses. The only way out of the cabin was through the door. We would be too exposed if we went out through there. I was equally certain they were not going to show themselves so I could get a shot at them.

We remained flat on the floor for a very long time. Fortunately, I'm good at playing the 'waiting game.' My biggest fear was, whoever it was would set the cabin on fire.

Mercy began to stir and went to the door and sniffed but did not growl. There was just enough starshine so I could see the door being pushed slightly inward. I had the gun in my hand and was ready, but the fact Mercy was not in a guarding stance had me puzzled. I heard a softly spoken word and knew why.

"Kate, it's Gary. Are you okay?"

I could feel my breathing slow and I relaxed my grip on the gun. "Yes, we're okay. What are you doing here? Stay down because I can't tell where the moron is who was shooting. We're on the floor."

Still speaking softly, he explained. "I was following a suspect when he headed this way. Then I lost him in the woods, but I strongly suspected he was on his way here. I saw the muzzle blast when he shot and made a move toward him. He took off at a dead run. I lost him then doubled back to check on you. Are you or the dogs hurt? If you can manage, I want to take you to the shore and hide you until I can come with a boat and pick you up. This situation is too dangerous for us to hike out right now. Can you do that?"

"We're fine to move, and I was going to when it seemed safer. He has night-vision and a really aggressive rifle. I figured he would set the building on fire next and shoot us when we came out. Let me grab our pack and we'll make a run for the shore. There's a cave in the rocks on the right-hand side of the path where we can hide and shelter."

I got across the floor and was just reaching for the pack-basket when another round hit the camp. It missed me by about a foot and I just dropped back down to the floor. So much for leaving. I knew both dogs were okay, but where was Gary?

"Gary, are you okay?"

"Yes, are you?"

"I am and the dogs are, but there isn't a chance in hell of us getting to the shore with him up there again."

"Kate, don't move, stay right where you are, I'm going up into the woods and see if I can rout him out. If you hear gunshots, get to shore and I'll find you after I finish with him."

I heard the sound of Gary moving around the camp, then no other noises. The cabin door was still ajar, and Mercy was lying just inside at full attention. I knew she could hear and see better than I could, so I was relying on her senses to alert me. Miss Joy was right by my side, but truly scared. So was I.

Time passes so slowly when you're waiting, especially in a situation where you have no control and cannot see or hear what is going on around you. It was still the middle of the night, so there wasn't any chance I could see anything for a few more hours. As I was lying there on the floor, I thought, *well you wanted a new adventure. Be careful what you wish for*. This was definitely not what I'd had in mind initially.

After what seemed like another whole lifetime, I heard a flurry of gunshots. I knew they were from Gary's gun, so I grabbed our pack basket and duffel along with the dogs on their leashes and we sprinted to the shore. I'm too damn old to be running while carrying stuff. My vision improved once we hit the shore due to the reflection of the night sky off the water. Thankfully, even though there was no moon, the sky was full of stars and no clouds. It was almost a high tide.

I turned to the right toward the cave we had seen on our earlier walks along the shore. I had never explored the interior. As we approached the entrance, Mercy began to growl. *Oh Lord, please don't let some animal be in there. We need a hiding place that is safe for a period of time.*

Mercy turned her body sideways, blocking the entrance while still emitting her odd growl. I moved her aside and was going to bend down to enter the opening when I got a whiff of the worse odor I had ever smelled. Something or someone was dead in there and had been for some time.

We were too exposed to be standing on the open beach and a great target for the shooter. I walked us to the edge of the woods where the rocks and the trees meet. We would be in shadows, and if we laid down, it would minimize our silhouettes. We might be okay at least until daylight.

Dawn was almost breaking when I heard a small boat coming into the cove. It was too dark to make out details, so we stayed where we were. The small outboard motor was cut, and the boat coasted onto the sand. When the lone occupant stepped out into the water's edge, I knew from the profile it was Gary.

He was walking straight to the cave when we stepped down off the rocks. His first words were, "I thought you were going to shelter in the cave where it was safe."

"Gary there's an issue with the cave. Do you have a flashlight with you? I think I may have found out what part of the problem here is. It had nothing to do with me, personally. This is a lot larger than we know. Take a look in the cave."

He walked forward and produced a small light. By the time he got within smelling distance of the entrance, he knew. He shined the light into the interior and stepped back. His only comment was, "Dear Lord."

He had extinguished the light. "I don't want you to see this. You are right, I need to call in some backup, this has gone way beyond my pay grade."

He pulled out his cell but had no reception on the beach. He climbed up on the rocks near where the woods began, but still had no signal. I watched as he walked up further on the path, still checking for signals on his phone. Finally, he stopped in the clearing of the path, and I could see he was talking with someone when I heard the whump of a bullet from that damn rifle.

I dropped to the sand and pulled the dogs down with me. I couldn't see Gary from this angle. I wrapped the dog's leashes around a loose rock, told them to stay and began crawling up over the rocks to see if I could spot him. I wouldn't make much of a night fighter, because when I can't see where to step, I sound like a herd of moose in the woods. I knew about where he was when I'd last seen him, so once I reached the path I belly-crawled toward the spot.

I found him lying on his back, shot in the shoulder and bleeding profusely. He still had his phone in his hand and someone was yelling on the other end of the transmission. I pulled the phone out of his hand and said, "I don't know who you are, but we need help here. Gary has been shot. He's down. Did he give you our location? I can't stay here because we have a lunatic trying to shoot us with a high-powered rifle with a silencer. I am going to try to move him to better cover."

The answer to this burst of information was predictable. "Who are you? What is going on there? Where are you?"

"To hell with who I am. Who are you and can you help us or get help to us right now? This is desperate."

"We are on the mainland and will be sending a Coast Guard boat at once, but we don't know your exact location."

"We're in a cove on the back side of the island, and a large boat can't get to us. I'm going to see if I can get him to the shore and perhaps into his small boat and far enough away from here so they can't shoot us. I need to stop this conversation and take care of him."

Gary began to moan, and I shushed him. He was losing a lot of blood. If I could pack the wound with something and get him onto his feet enough to get him out of the clearing, perhaps I could keep him somewhat safe until help arrived.

He was trying to speak, "Get the hell out of here. Take the boat and go, or they will kill you. Don't argue with me...just go."

"Gary, shut up, and try to help me get you out of this clearing and out of range. Can you do that if I help you? I'm going to rip off a piece of your shirt and stuff the wound. It is going to hurt like the dickens, but it'll perhaps stop the flow of blood."

His only response was, "Go now."

Not happening. I was taking him with me, one way or the other. I tore off a hunk of his shirt and ripped it into two pieces. I stuffed one portion into the hole I could see on his front side then pushed him over on his side and repeated the process on his back side. Now to try to get him up without us getting hit again.

I'm not sure if I heard, or just sensed, someone near me, but the hair on the back of my head was standing straight up when I saw a blur out of the corner of my eye. The next noise I heard was a death-defying growl as Mercy lunged over me and Gary, making body contact with someone. My first reaction was, I didn't have my gun. I realized Gary's gun was in his holster. I unsnapped the strap, yanking it out. I had no time to consider what it was or anything. I prayed the safety was not on. Mercy had the person on the ground and he was trying to stab her with a knife. I jumped away from Gary pointed and pulled the trigger.

The man screamed, Mercy backed away and I grabbed his rifle. I had no idea where the knife had gone. I held the gun on him and was prepared to kill him if necessary. He had scared us, hurt Gary, and then tried to harm my dog. All good reasons in my book to kill him right there and right now.

"Don't even breathe, or you never will again." He didn't even twitch. Lucky for him, because when I get to that state, I don't have even one ounce of backup. I would shoot him dead with no regrets.

Gary was trying to roll over so he could get up. I wasn't sure how I could assist him and keep stupid down. When he rolled over, I noticed he had a set of handcuffs on his belt. If I could cuff stupid, with Mercy's assistance, I would be able to help Gary.

I saw Mercy still had her leash on. I unhooked it and, with some instructions from Gary, handcuffed stupid, then I tied him to a tree with her leash around his neck while he kept screaming that he was shot and would bleed to death. Like I cared. My only regret was I didn't have anything to gag him with.

Now what should I do? Where is the freaking playbook when you need it?

Mercy turned and dashed toward the shoreline. I had forgotten Miss Joy was still tied to the rock and was all alone. I passed Gary stupid's rife and told him to shoot if he needed to. I still had Gary's gun and I dashed after Mercy.

When I got to the top of the bank, I saw a small boat edging into the shore beside the boat Gary had arrived in. Somehow, I knew this was not the assistance I had hoped for. Why would a person with a motor on the stern be quietly paddling to shore?

There was no point in going back to tell Gary. He was not going to be of any help at this point. I very carefully stayed in the treeline while I watched the action play out on the beach. The person was stepping out of the boat and pulling it ashore. He had not spotted our stuff or the dogs yet. He was carrying what looked like one of the black construction site trash bags. He was striding directly to the cave. He was a man on a mission, to be certain.

Mercy was busy watching him while tugging Miss Joys leash free from the rock where I had tied her. When she had accomplished the task, she took the leash in her mouth and pulled Miss Joy in my direction. Once Miss Joy understood where she was going, she hopped up onto the rocks and came to my side.

I patted Mercy, took Miss Joy to Gary and told her to stay. I told him someone was trying to remove the body from the cave. I was not about to let that happen. Whatever this mess was all about, it had impacted me, and I wanted it over. I took Mercy and we headed for the beach.

I was becoming alarmed because there were too many players now and only me with no backup. This could get really bad very quickly. Too late now; I was too involved to stop.

Mercy and I followed the path. Then, when we were on the sand, we crept along quietly until we could see the mouth of the cave. We waited. Whoever was in there was in a hurry and not being too quiet. I could hear the bag being shaken out and some muffled cussing. When the sounds changed to something being dragged on the sand. I paused to let them get outside of the cave so they had no protection to bolt back in and shoot at me then I spoke. "Stop right where you are and don't move."

The person froze in his tracks, dropped his hold on the bag and swung his arm to his side. I wasn't taking a chance...I fired a shot at his leg. He screamed and bent over to grab his leg. I hollered, "Stand up and put your hands in the air or the next shot will be in your neck."

He stood as well as he could with the injury to his leg, but put only one hand in the air. I was certain he had a gun or another weapon. I wasn't going to give him a chance to use it. I was ready to send off another shot. He saw I was serious and quickly raised his other arm. I saw in the process of being startled and shot, he'd dropped his gun in the sand. Good, end of that concern. "Step away from the weapon. Do it now!" He was reluctant, but he moved to the side, dragging his injured leg with him.

Now I had another problem. Another person to keep still and nothing to tie them up with. I remembered the old punt they had trashed was still on the shore in a pile. There had been a piece of rope on the prow. I didn't know if I could even untie it, but I had to do something. I began backing toward the damaged punt and stupid number two thought he saw an opportunity, lowered his arms, and was gauging how fast he could grab his gun off the sand. I was ready to fire another shot at him when Mercy took charge by getting between him and the gun. She was growling with bared teeth just to keep him reminded of who was in charge.

I found the rope, but knew I had nothing to get it free with when I realized it wasn't an issue.

I made him hobble to the pile of rubble and tied him hand and foot, damaged leg and all, to the pile. If he decided to make a run for freedom, he would have to tow part of a boat with him.

I left Mercy to guard him and ran back to see how Gary was doing. Not good. He had lost quite a bit of blood, and he wasn't a young man. I could see he was still able to speak, so I asked him what I should do. He offered me a faltering lopsided grin and managed to say, "Why are you asking me now? So far I think you have this situation under control."

"Can you get any cell coverage at all? Who were you talking with when this thing fell apart? Do you think they have sent any assistance?"

He looked really weak, but I had to know. He rallied and managed a few words. "Sheriff's office on mainland. Sending a boat should be here soon. They can get into the cove. Coast Guard behind them. Will you be okay till they come?"

"I will, but how about you? What can I do to help you? I know this is stupid to ask at a time like this, but do you have another clip for this pistol with you?"

He almost laughed then muttered, "You ask the darndest questions of any woman I ever met. Can you reach inside my pocket and get one? Watch for the boat. They promised there would be an EMT on board, and I really think I need one."

I made one last check of stupid and made certain he was still tied securely to the tree, then dashed off to check on stupid number two. As I looked back, Miss Joy was licking Gary's cheek as if to tell him to hang in there for a little longer.

When I got to the beach, I could hear a high-powered boat coming and worried if it could get into the cove as the tide was going out and the water would be shallower. I needn't have worried...it was an air boat. Not what I would have expected. Then a sudden panicky thought. What if this was not help but more of the bandits? Some days you just can't catch a break, and I hadn't been on a hot streak this week. I would be ready, no matter what we had come this far.

The boat swooped into the cove and was beached on the sand in a matter of seconds. Well, if they were not the good guys, I was way outgunned. Each had a rifle, and they were all wearing sidearms. One was carrying a medic's box along with a folding stretcher. Thank God, the troops had arrived. I could breathe again. I just prayed they were in time for Gary.

I showed the medic where Gary was, and he began taking care of him. They rushed him to the boat and whisked him offshore. The others needed answers, and I was the only one there. One of the men introduced himself as Mike. If he gave me a last name or rank, I didn't catch it.

I tried to give him a thumbnail sketch of what had happened. Other than lots of jokes about my containment systems with the others on the team, they seemed to understand.

The missing link to the mess was who was in the black bag. I had no clue, nor did I wish to know. I was done with this adventure.

Nine

If I thought I was finished with the saga, I was deluding myself. Mike and his crew helped me with loading the dogs and my gear onto their boat when it returned from delivering Gary to the Coast Guard cutter. They took us to the mainland but wouldn't allow us to get my truck or go home.

I was correct when I had told Gary this was a lot bigger than we could imagine. I didn't have a clue of the magnitude of the issue.

When Mike informed me I was not free to leave, I think my brain finally clicked on to the fact they had no witnesses to any of the drama other than me. I asked Mike a simple question, "Why are you holding me? Am I under arrest? I need some facts here. Should I be calling a lawyer or what?"

Mike looked like he would rather be talking with the devil himself instead of me. "I can only tell you what I know. Gary is the senior officer on this case, and his last words to me were 'don't release her to go home,' and he passed out.

"He is in surgery right now and won't be able to speak with us until the doctors say so. Until then, I am going to detain you. You are not under arrest, and I don't want to put you under arrest. I need you to stay here with us. We have a set of quarters for when we need to stay over, and I'm going to put you there. It may be a couple of days before Gary can assist us with what he wanted. I will make certain you are comfortable and fed. You can walk the dogs in the attached lawn area by the back door. All you need to do is buzz us if you want to go out or if you need something. I am truly sorry. I know it has been a tough time for you."

His mouth was saying the right words, but there was no warmth or compassion in any of it. With his speech out of the way, he led me to a corridor with a locked door and walked me past several steel doors to one at the end of a hall. He unlocked the door and carried our stuff inside, placing it on the floor. When he left, it was evident he had locked us in.

The space was pleasant enough, I guess, if you don't mind being locked up. There was a full bathroom with clean towels, soap, shampoo, etc. There was a full-sized bed, a chair that was a recliner, a wall hung television, and a table with three wooden chairs. There were windows with blinds that looked out onto the postage stamp lawn. The grassy space was fenced with a high security fence with razor wire all along the top. Gee, how friendly, I thought...just like home.

My first instinct was to panic. However, I would have bet my last dollar the place was covered with surveillance equipment, and the last thing I wanted was to give any indication of emotion they could use against me for whatever reason. I had no idea what they were holding me for, other than at Gary's request. Whatever that meant.

I rustled around in my pack basket and the duffle for what I hoped was at least one pair of clean underwear, a shirt, and a clean pair of jeans. The one thing I was going to do was take advantage of the shower to clean up and brush my teeth. I hadn't had a warm soapy shower for several days.

To say I enjoyed a long hot shower would be an understatement.

While I was using up all of the hot water I wanted and their shampoo, I had a personal chuckle. They had no idea I had not only Gary's pistol in the bottom of the pack basket with his extra clip, I also had my own revolver. I sure wasn't going to buzz them to share the information.

I made sure when I finished my shower I dressed in the bathroom. There was so much steam, any camera lens would be unable to distinguish anything other than shadows.

When I came out of the bathroom, I fixed a water dish for the dogs and gave them some treats. None of us had eaten anything since the night before. I was hungry, and I was sure they were.

I found the buzzer Mike mentioned next to what looked like an intercom. I pushed it and waited. A male voice spoke. "How may I help you?"

"I haven't had any food or drink since last night, so I was wondering if perhaps I could send out for something, or you could supply me with a meal and some coffee, soda and water."

It took a few minutes, then the voice returned, "What would you like to eat? We can send you down some coffee and bottled water right away. If you look in the small fridge by the table, there may be sodas in there."

I hadn't even noticed the fridge. I walked over and opened the door. He was correct; there was water in bottles and several cans of soda. I walked back to the intercom. "I'm not very fussy as long as it is something to eat, and coffee would be great. I found the water and the sodas, so I'm fine with that. Thank you."

"I will have your food and coffee in about fifteen to twenty minutes. Are you sure you don't have something you would prefer?"

"Nope. If I don't have to catch it, kill it, or cook it, I'll be happy."

I swear I heard him laugh when I finished. Once I began thinking about food, I was starved. How strange was that? I fed the dogs some kibble and we sat down to wait for whatever would come next.

In less than the twenty minutes he had told me, there was a knock on the door and the sound of a key turning in the lock. A sharp looking young man came in with a tray containing a bag, two cups of coffee, and a big smile.

"Hi there, my name is Josh and I will be serving you tonight. I hope this will be satisfactory for now. We will serve regular dinner about six."

I didn't know what was in the bag, but the smell was enticing. My stomach began to growl and I was ready to eat anything, including the bag and any napkins, if they were there. "Thanks, Josh, I appreciate your service and delivery. Do you think I could get you to open the door so I can take the dogs outside?"

"Certainly. I can leave it open so they can come in and out if you want. You may get some bugs because the door doesn't have a screen. No one can see into the yard, and no one will bother you or the dogs. If you need anything else, just buzz me."

"Thank you. Have you had any word on how Gary is doing yet? He took quite a hit and lost a lot of blood."

His reply was guarded, "We haven't heard anything yet. I will let you know if I hear anything. By the way, there will be nothing about any of that mission on the nightly news, so don't be alarmed."

Hmm, alarmed? Why would I be alarmed? I devoured the best large greasy hamburger with lettuce, tomato, and mayo I had ever seen and then shared the French fries with the dogs.

I let them out to do their thing and left the door closed but not locked. I pushed the recliner back and tried to find something on the television to watch and take my mind of the current situation. When I woke up, for a moment I had no idea what time it was or where I was. I must have been exhausted because I never nap in the daytime. Miss Joy was in my lap, and Mercy was sound asleep at my feet.

I wasn't certain what had jarred me awake. It couldn't have been anything too awful because neither of the dogs had barked. I would just sit here for a few moments and collect my bearings.

After a trip to the bathroom, I dug out my cell to check the time. It was late in the day. I had been asleep for over three hours. Although I had my cell and enough bars, I didn't want to use it to make any calls until I knew what was going on. The kids didn't think I would be back for a couple of days, anyway.

The dogs and I watched some television, ate the dinner Josh brought down, and managed to get some restless sleep that night. I am not a person who likes being confined, even when I'm home or in my own space. I knew I would have to make the best of what I had because it was Sunday and there was no way I could contact an attorney or anyone else who had any authority.

I buzzed Josh to see if there was any word on Gary yet and to find why he wanted me held. I was ready to be home. When he answered, I inquired about the status of Gary's condition.

Josh's answer was polite, but again somewhat guarded, "Gary survived the surgery and has not been able to contact us yet. I am sure we will know more by tomorrow."

I resigned myself to the fact that the man had been shot, had undergone some surgery, was not a young man, and most likely was in pain and heavily medicated. My situation would not be on the top of his priority list for sure.

Later in the day, Josh buzzed me on the intercom. "If you are up to it, Mike would like to speak with you. May he come down?"

What a silly request; it was their jail I was locked up in. "Certainly."

When Mike entered the room, he seemed uncomfortable. That made me uneasy, to say the least. He had a pad of paper and what looked like a small recorder.

We sat at the table and just kind of looked each other over for a few minutes. The procedure reminded me of two wolves squaring off. I didn't know what he was looking for and, for some reason, I didn't trust him as I had Gary.

When he spoke, his voice was not comforting because he didn't seem to have a set direction he wanted to go. "Do you mind if I take some notes? I would rather record our conversation, if possible."

I became really leery of him and I wasn't sure why. The only thing I knew for certain was my leery meter had kept me alive for a lot of years and I respected it. "I'm not comfortable with you recording anything. To be quite honest, I would rather discuss this whole thing with Gary. He knows what happened and I would guess he knows the why of it also."

I saw a flash of anger in Mike's eyes, which I'm sure he didn't have a clue I'd picked up on. Now I didn't trust him at all. I may have made a horrible mistake with my comment, but I was going to stand by it. If necessary, I would contact a lawyer to handle whatever this mess was. So far, I didn't have a clue. I did know I was done with Mike.

His next comment sealed the deal for me. "Well Gary won't be released from the hospital for some time to come. He will have sick leave to recover, so you may be staying here for a long damn time. Because of your attitude, it may be necessary to move you to a cell and the dogs can't go there. I guess that's your choice. Think about it." With that being said, he stomped out of the room.

Ten

It was time for me to get some reinforcements. I fished around in my pack, grabbed my cell, then I wrapped it in a shirt and headed for the outside. I knew without any doubt Mike would be monitoring my actions and I wasn't going to help him. Once outside, I fished out the card Gary had given me on the island and texted his cell number. I was not certain he would even have it with him in the hospital.

My message was short and sweet, '*need help now. bad stuff is happening. do not contact anyone here.*'

I slid the phone under my shirt and prayed like I hadn't prayed in a long time. I needed help only God could provide at the moment.

Something was very wrong here at the jail.

Time passed and I didn't hear from Gary. I was trying to figure out my next move when I heard the lock on the door being opened. It was Josh. I started to relax when I heard someone yelling. It was Mike and, because of the length of the corridor and the solidness of the walls, it amplified the sound like a megaphone. Mike yelled, "Get out of here!" Dear Lord, I recognized his voice as the man who had been piloting the boat which tried to run over us in the cove the other day. Now I was really scared.

Josh looked as confused as I was. He turned and spoke quietly, "Sir, I was just bringing her a snack because dinner is always late on Sunday."

Mike hustled into the room and curtly dismissed Josh by taking the tray from his hand and plunking it down on the table, then stomping out while herding Josh up the hall. I heard him say as the door was closing, "I thought I told you she was in isolation. That means she gets nothing unless I approve it."

A new dimension of stress was now added. I knew it would be impossible for me to get to anyone today and would need to wait until tomorrow to reach an attorney. My spirits sank to a new low. I know when I'm outgunned.

I was sitting on one of the chairs in the back area with the dogs when my phone vibrated. It startled me because in all the flap with Mike and Josh, I'd forgotten it. I didn't want anyone to see I was using it, so I bent over and pretended to be patting the dogs. Thank God, it was Gary.

His first words were, "Are you okay? Are the dogs with you? What do you need?"

"Gary, I can't talk long. We have a big problem here. First, I need to tell you Mike was the person running the boat who tried to run me down. He has refused to let Josh come in here and has put me in isolation. He's threatening to move me to a cell and take the dogs. I don't think he knows I recognized who he is, but he doesn't want me to talk to anyone. I told him I would only speak with you, and he informed me that would be weeks away, but in the meantime, he would incarcerate me. I'm sorry to bother you, but I need immediate assistance. Can you at least get me an attorney or someone who can get us released from here?"

"Help is on the way. The surgery went fine, and it is not the first gunshot wound I've had. It will take us about an hour to get there. Sit tight. Keep the phone hidden. Don't tell anyone we talked."

I took a deep breath. It seemed I hadn't breathed in a long time. I continued to play and pat the dogs as I carefully slid the phone back into my waistband.

I wandered over to the table to see what was on the tray. It was a sandwich wrapped in Saran wrap, a small bag of chips and a cup of hot water with a tea bag on the top. Josh had also included a cookie.

I shared the sandwich and chips with the dogs as I was running low on their kibble. The tea tasted like the nectar of the gods. I'm much too old for this much stress.

I tried to be patient waiting for Gary to arrive. I didn't want to seem anxious and give away the fact he was coming. I had a really awful thought: what if Mike would not let Gary in to see me? I had no idea of his status here at the jail. I would wait and pray because I didn't think I could handle another problem.

An eternity passed, or at least it seemed like one, when I heard the lock on the door being turned. My heart rate accelerated to stroke level. I could hear the mummer of voices but could not distinguish any words. The door began to open slowly and my heart sank because I recognized Mike's voice saying, "I am not going to allow this, regardless of what you say."

The next voice I heard was Gary's. "This is out of your hands and, if you want to question that, go see who's sitting out front in the mobile unit. Now get the hell out of my way."

In the next instant, I'm not positive what happened: either Gary stumbled or he was shoved, but he came close to falling on the floor. I had been standing so close to the door that I caught him and was able to keep him upright. Mike was right behind him, and hate was etched on his face like a mask. I held onto Gary to steady him.

I lead him to the recliner while Mercy stood guard between him and Mike. I worried Mike would hurt Mercy if she lunged at him. He was armed.

Gary was trying to move his arm that was not in the sling to get something out of his shirt pocket. I wanted to be helpful, so I offered to reach for him. It was his phone. He opened it and pushed a button then snapped it shut, returning it to his pocket.

Out in the hallway, all hell broke loose. I could hear feet running down the length of it and shouting. Either assistance was here, or they were having a jail break. I didn't care which.

The door was pushed the rest of the way open with such force it slammed into the wall with a crash. Three men in full riot gear were in the room together so rapidly I couldn't think of how they all got through the doorway at once.

Gary spoke to one of the men. "Take him out of here, disarm him, and lock him in solitary. We will only be a matter of minutes before we'll be ready to leave."

He turned his attention to me. "Pack up your stuff and the dogs. We're out of here."

Blessed words to my ears. I was packed and the dogs leashed before I think I even exhaled. The remaining man grabbed our stuff, and I took the dogs.

We departed the jail and were escorted to a large, ugly, black transport vehicle. There was plenty of room for all of us, including the dogs. When the door closed, the driver nodded to Gary and we were off, to where I hadn't a clue. I knew it would be a far safer place than the jail had been.

My attention turned to Gary. "Are you okay? Are you supposed to be out and being pushed around? I need to thank you for coming; it was getting dicey back there."

"I'll be fine once I get you to a safer place. I told them not to release you to go home because I knew they would try to kill you, thinking you could identify any one of them. I didn't realize at the time I'd put the hare into the fox's den."

My jaw dropped. "I wouldn't have ever recognized Mike because I hadn't seen his face the day of the boat incident. When he came in to interview me, he seemed unnecessarily nervous. But it was his voice when he yelled down the hallway at Josh. Now that you have him, can I go home and enjoy some peace and quiet? I've had quite enough adventure for now."

His reply scared me. "No, you can't, Mike is just a small-time player in this mess. I listened to you when you said this was bigger than just a murder on the island. Remember at that time, there was only one body we knew about there. I made several phone calls and rounded up facts and figures, none of which made any sense until we all compared our notes. I'm going to take you to the only safe place I know at the moment. You and the pups will be safe and secure, and not locked up in a facility."

"Gary, I appreciate your assistance, but I don't have supplies for the dogs or clothing for me to be gone from my home any longer. I also have lawn care that needs to be done and the house looked after. I live alone, so there isn't anyone to tend to those things."

He nodded and smiled. "I know more about you and your living situation than you could ever imagine. The lawn has been mowed, the house checked out, and I have plenty of your clothing all packed and enough dog food and favorite toys so they will be fine. I also have your favorite wine and munchies with us. Don't worry...you are now in good hands."

I was flabbergasted. I wondered who he'd talked to. I was truly afraid to ask. So much for thinking I was anonymous.

My turn to grin. "Well, you do know I still have your service pistol and the clips. I figured with everything going south in the jail, I just wouldn't tell them. They also didn't ask."

We rode in silence. Then when we arrived at a dirt road which was very rutty and looked deserted, the vehicle bumped along, I could see Gary wince at every jostle. I knew he was in a lot of pain.

"It's obvious you are really uncomfortable and your shoulder is hurting. Why are you doing this?"

I got a lopsided grin and a stoic reply. "It's my job, madam, we must keep you safe until this mess is cleared up. We are almost done with this washboard they consider a road. Don't try this road in that lady-truck you drive."

I had not a clue where we were. I did know I wasn't frightened, and the dogs were sound asleep in the back, so if they were not worried, I really didn't care. They were great indicators of danger. Well, Mercy was. Miss Joy, not so much.

We survived the trek through the alder swamp with mud halfway up the wheels and came out to a sandy beach area. We were ushered out, and while the dogs did their thing and explored, the men unloaded our stuff and other packages from the back. Gary led the way to a small metal skiff beached behind some rocks.

The men moved the small boat into the water and began to load everything into it. There certainly wasn't room for the dogs or Gary and me. We stood and watched as two of the men pushed off and rowed away. Interesting, where were they going?

A short time later, the skiff reappeared with only one man on board. Gary smiled. "Our turn now."

We boarded the boat and the man rowed away without a word. It just occurred to me, Gary had never introduced me to any of these men or them to me. I wondered why. Someday my curiosity was going to be the death of me. When I was a kid, my dad had often voiced the same opinion.

When we went around the curve of the rocks, there was an ordinary looking lobster fishing boat waiting with the engine running. The man rowed us to the stern where there was a platform of sorts. The guy on board assisted us in scrambling aboard. Mercy was easy… she just jumped from the skiff to the platform, then onto the stern and down to the deck. Miss Joy needed to be lifted out, up and over. Next, it was my turn. Not an issue, but both men were offering assistance. Gary brought up the rear. When we were all aboard, the man who had rowed returned to the skiff and rowed back to land.

The boat began to move smoothly over the water as we found seating in the cabin. Miss Joy sat on my lap while Mercy laid at my feet. I was totally lost. I had no idea where we were or where we were going. The thought that perhaps I was gullible for going off on this leg of the journey without knowing any more than I did briefly crossed my mind.

I was getting worried about Gary. He was looking deathly pale and I knew he was experiencing a lot of pain. The man piloting the boat kept glancing at him but said nothing.

We were on the trip for what seemed like a long time. Off in the distance, I could see a small island. Again, I had no idea where we were or what island it was. It appeared to be heavily wooded with what looked like spruce trees. The coastline was rocky, which is typical of islands in this part of the state. When we got closer, the boat slowed and we swung around to the other part of the island. I was surprised to see a sheltered cove with a pier and a small sandy beach. If you didn't know it was there, you could sail right on by as it appeared to be just a rocky shoreline.

The man at the helm brought us into the pier smoothly and secured the boat's lines to the cleats with no effort. You would have thought he did this every day as a matter of course. For all I knew, he very well could.

He helped me to disembark with Miss Joy in my arms. Mercy was already on the wharf waiting. Gary was having a problem getting up from where he was sitting. The man jumped back aboard to assist him. I heard Gary murmur quietly, "Dana, I'm okay, take care of them, please."

Now I had a name with the face, so I used it, "Dana, what can I do to assist you?"

Dana looked slightly confused as he glanced from me to Gary, but he agreed assistance was needed. "I need to go get the cart and the four-wheeler so we can move him and the supplies. Do you mind just staying with him? I'll only be a matter of a few minutes."

"Of course not, go do what you need to. I'll stay right here with him. Does he have any meds for the pain?"

Dana smiled, shook his head and said, "He does but he wouldn't take any until he was sure you were safely here and taken care of. I won't be long." I knew he meant the last statement because he took off on a dead run toward a path leading away from the shore.

I sat next to Gary and could see he was sweating from the pain and the effort to stay sitting up. "Why don't you stretch out on the seat and rest for a few minutes until he returns? Do you have any water so you could take some of your meds now? It isn't smart to let the pain get ahead of the meds. I'll stay right here with you."

Gary seemed to consider my suggestion, "I have pills in my pocket and there is water on a shelf forward."

Thank God he was going to comply. Even if we had to carry him off the boat, it was better than seeing anyone in so much pain. I grabbed a bottle of water off the shelf and fished out the vial of pills. I lifted his head and held the water. When he had swallowed the dose, I don't know who was more relieved, him or me.

He laid back on the seat. I pulled off my sweatshirt and rolled it up to make a pillow and slid it under his head. In a few minutes, I could see his body beginning to relax with color starting to return to his face. He was no longer sweating. I wished I had a light blanket to cover him. This day had been extremely busy and much too long for a person just out of the hospital after surgery for a bad wound.

What was making it worse for me was that I felt it was my fault he had been shot in the first place. I knew it wasn't a rational thought, but I always maintained because I was brought up Catholic it had to be my fault. Born in the womb and driven by guilt. Perhaps I got it from my Irish mother.

I heard the sounds of an engine, so I assumed it was Dana with whatever conveyance he had run off to procure. Gary was resting comfortably and I hated to disturb him.

Dana came onto the wharf with the machine and a small cart. He looked really anxious. I walked over to the side of the boat and told him Gary had taken some medicine and seemed to be resting. I offered to help him unload the supplies and our gear for the first trip. Then, if we were careful, we could move Gary, and the dogs and I would walk. He considered it, agreeing it might be the best plan.

Again, I stayed with Gary while Dana made the round trip. While he was gone, the radio on the boat began to crackle and someone sent a call signal. Gary was asleep so I did nothing.

When Dana returned, I told him about the transmission. He stepped aboard and activated the radio. I went to the stern so he could converse in private.

When Dana came out on the deck, he looked concerned. My first question was, "What's wrong, Dana?"

He hesitated for a moment, and I could tell he was having a personal struggle with how much to share with me. When he spoke, I understood why. "I'm not sure how we're going to transport Gary in the condition he's in without doing any damage to his shoulder. If

I put him in the cart, I am worried I will jostle him too much. I can't leave him here, and he can't ride on the back of the ATV."

"How far do we need to take him? Could you and I carry him if we make a stretcher?"

Dana thought about my suggestion for a few seconds, then told me the obvious. "He is a large man, he would be dead weight, and you're a woman. The trail goes uphill."

I laughed. "Sorry about that…I already knew those facts except for how far. Do you think we should take him back to the hospital?"

No thought required for Dana's answer. "No, he would kill me if I left you here alone, and he would not want to be 'kept' someplace against his will."

Okay. "Let's make a stretcher. All we need are a couple of poles and a blanket. We might have to rest a bit on the way up, but we can do this."

It took us the better part of a half hour to rig up a stretcher, but we managed with only one extra trip to wherever Dana had been going. Gary was out like a light and didn't even moan as we loaded him onto the makeshift transporter. Just as well.

Dana had found a sheet of plywood and screws in the workshop, so we attached it to two long poles. We set the stretcher on the deck and carefully picked Gary up, mattress and all, and set him on it. The next step was to see if we could lift him onto the gunnel of the boat. With our first lift, we knew we could move him with just the two of us. We got him off the gunnel and began the trek up the path.

We decided to carry him for a distance, then stop, and Dana would run back down the trail and get the ATV with the cart. Dana said the worse part of the path was the bottom, where it was the steepest and had sustained some washouts from recent heavy rain storms.

We managed to get a good distance up the path before we took our second rest-break. I breathed and sat for the few minutes it took Dana to get down and back. I was really too old for this exercise, but I was also too stubborn to quit.

Dana was funny when we were picking Gary's stretcher up again. "I am going to tell him he needs to diet when he wakes up. Do you think you can still do this?"

"Sure. If he gets too heavy, I'll take his shoes off. That will lighten the load. He must wear a size fourteen, for Heaven's sake."

We trudged, and I do mean trudged, what seemed to be straight up the trail for another few minutes. He was getting heavier with each step. When this happens to me if I'm climbing a mountain, I play a mental game with myself and think of something I really want, then imagine it at the head of the trail. Right then, I wanted a Diet Coke.

Dana was also out of breath, but managed to say, "If we can go another twenty feet, I think I can transport him the rest of the way with the cart. Can you hold out that long?"

A carrot! "Oh sure, no problem. I'll schedule my heart attack for later."

We reached a small clearing and carefully set the stretcher down. With a short rest stop, we caught our breath and Dana ran back down the trail to get the equipment. I looked around and the path still wound upward but seemed much smoother because it was a large ledge.

When Dana returned, we placed the stretcher across the cart. He drove at a crawl while I steadied the load. It was much easier for us physically, but it still took some time before we rounded a bend in the trail, and I could see the roofline of a structure sitting just below the crest of the ledge. We would make it.

Dana was able to get us within steps of the door, so once he got it opened, we picked up the stretcher only to find it wouldn't fit through the opening. We set Gary down, picked him up with the pad and carried him into a bedroom. We decided rather than jostle and shake him any more we would leave him on the pad and just cover him with a blanket.

I prayed we had not harmed him with all the moving. Although we had been careful, we had still bumped him around substantially. I hadn't checked the bottle of pills to see what they were, and he had only taken one. I was worried about his condition, even though he seemed to be breathing normally. I would keep a close eye on him. If anything changed, whether he liked it or not, we would take him back to the hospital, although the thought of carrying him back to the boat nearly gave me heart failure.

I drew a deep breath and began to assess our surroundings. It was an adorable cottage with views of the ocean from every room. I realized it was totally off the grid. I had seen solar panels on the roof; running water from a spring piped into the house supplied a full bathroom. There was a very functional kitchen, a large living room with a woodburning fireplace. I found all of our stuff in the other bedroom.

Dana was sitting on the outside deck drinking a beer. He looked like he was exhausted as well as concerned. He was still wearing his gun belt, and I noticed he had a pair of binoculars and an assault rifle beside him.

When I went out onto the deck, he grinned and said, "Just another day on the job. Don't worry...this place has more security measures than you could ever imagine in your wildest dreams. You just can't be too careful nowadays. Do you think Gary is okay?"

"I checked on him and his breathing seems normal. I'm not a medic, but I think as long as he's resting comfortably, we should let him be. I will keep checking in on him. Rest is the best cure for him right now. I'm certain he signed himself out of the hospital."

Dana nodded, then informed me of the preparations that had been made prior to our arriving here. "There's all kinds of food in the fridge and cupboards. There are also dog food and treats. You will find your favorite wine out there, and you might want to have a glass and relax before I start dinner. It has been a long day for you. The dogs can roam freely because there isn't anyone else on this property. I also don't think there is any wildlife, other than the gulls."

I did go find the wine and poured myself a glass. We were sitting on the deck watching the sun beginning to set when Mercy lifted her head and gave me the soft woof she does when she is trying to get my attention. I followed her gaze and was surprised to see Gary standing there. He was upright, but a little unsteady. Dana and I both jumped up at once to help him into a chair.

I was the first to speak. "Why are you up walking around? How do you feel? Can I get something for you?"

He rewarded my inquisition with a grin. "I didn't want to miss the cocktail hour. After all, I am supposed to be the host. How in God's world did you guys get me up here? I last remember being on the boat. What happened?"

My turn to have some fun. "I drugged you. You should be more careful about who gives you pills. We will probably never tell you how we got you here. I'm just grateful we didn't kill you in the process. Now, can I get you something to either eat or drink?"

"A bottle of water would be great. Thanks, guys. However you did it, I'm happy to be here. Now perhaps I can recover."

I brought Gary his water, then the three of us sat in comfortable silence with the dogs. There was a slight breeze, so no bugs, and it was still warm enough to sit without a shirt on. Sometimes life just feels good, and anyone is a fool if they don't enjoy the moment. Sometimes a 'moment' is all you have.

<h1 style="text-align:center">Eleven</h1>

Gary looked at Dana and asked, "Where is Rob? Will he come up to eat with us?"

Dana shook his head and spoke quietly. "He isn't here, and he isn't coming. When I got back to the boat after the first trip to get the ATV, there had been a transmission on the radio. I called back on our channel, and Rob told me both he and Sam had been reassigned. When I inquired why, he told me they didn't feel you needed that level of coverage. To quote him, he said, 'you had only an elderly woman, two dogs, Dana and yourself. If between the two of you, you couldn't handle it, you should put in for early retirement.' End of the conversation. What do you want me to do? I secured the boat on our last trip up here. I don't want to alarm you, but I'm not happy to be short-handed here right now."

Gary straightened in his chair and a scowl crossed his face. I could sense certainly he was not comfortable with the news Dana just delivered. He pondered the information for another few minutes, then declared, "Those idiots! We're sitting ducks here without at least one more person." It was very apparent there was more going on than I knew. "Have you had a chance to check on the security cameras and the sensors?"

Dana shook his head. "Not yet. We haven't been up here at the house for long. I'll walk down and check the trailside, then do a perimeter search. Let me get the radios. If you should need to, can you shoot with your left hand?"

"I can, and Kate is also a good shot. Will you please get a couple of rifles out with the ammo just in case we need them?"

Uneasiness filled my bones. It was the same mess, just a different location with different players. My mind asked, "How do you continue to get into these situations?" I had no rational answer at that point. My database was flat.

Dana returned with two rifles with scopes, two boxes of shells and two extra clips for each. He handed Gary a small handheld radio and a larger phone.

Gary nodded and took the phone. It resembled what I would call a 'field combat phone.' As Dana was bringing equipment out onto the deck, the dogs began to get anxious. I didn't know if they were picking up on our attitudes or if they knew something we didn't.

Gary had connected with someone on his call. I wanted to give him space to converse, so I headed for the inside of the cottage. But not before I heard him say, "What in hell were you thinking? We're sitting ducks out here without men. I don't think you are understanding the gravity of what is going on. I need at least two men here with me, plus Dana. This was all arranged when we left. Who changed the orders and why?"

He appeared to be listening to the transmission but was waving me back to the deck.

"You listen to me. I don't give a sweet damn who told you what, I want to be connected with Reilly right now. I don't care where he went, you find him and get him to contact me right now. This is urgent! Do you understand me?"

Gary looked at me, then at Dana. "Guys, I may have made a bad mistake. The plan was all in place, and, for some reason, it has been changed. We have the three of us for now, and I'm concerned we will have issues during the night. Kate, if you want, I can have Dana take you and the dogs back to the mainland. I don't know where you will be safe there. I'm truly sorry. The decision is up to you. I know where there are hiding places here on the island, but I can't guarantee anyone else doesn't know where they are. Dana, the same goes for you. This is a mess, and I'm not going to dismiss it lightly. You both need to make up your minds. I'm going to stay here, because, truthfully, I don't know if I can make the return trip right now."

Dana and I answered as if in one voice. "We're not leaving you here alone."

That was settled. Now, I would go see if I could rustle up something for supper. I fed the dogs and let them roam about a little, then returned to the kitchen. I wasn't up to producing a feast, but I could at least feed us.

Gary stayed on the deck, which was okay, because I could still see him from the kitchen window. Dana had walked off into the surrounding woods with his radio and his rifle. Miss Joy was sitting on the deck with Gary, and Mercy was with me.

By the time Dana reappeared, I had food ready. We ate in strained silence. Whoever Gary wanted to speak with had not returned his call.

While I was cleaning up the kitchen and doing the dishes, Dana announced he would be gone for a while and we were not to be concerned. He had the radio with him, and if there was an issue, he would let us know. He offered to assist Gary to get him into bed before he left. All he got for his effort was a rebuff.

Before Dana left, he took me into the small room off the kitchen and showed me the radio transmitters and the screens for the surveillance cameras and sensors. He also explained the alarm system. If someone touched any one of the many trip wires installed around the property, it would beep and give a location on the screen. He showed me how to contact him on the small radio he had hooked to his shirt.

I had been watching Gary closely, and I could see fatigue was taking a toll on his body. It was almost dusk, so I went out and convinced him to come into the house and, at the very least, lie on his bed. I promised him I would wake him if anything happened. He had placed his service pistol on his nightstand. He also had the radio and the large phone with him. So much for a peaceful and restful convalescence. He did allow me to leave the small lamp turned on so I could check on him. However, he would not take any additional pain meds, no matter how insistently I urged him.

I left the small light on in the kitchen and took the dogs out onto the deck to sit for a few minutes. I had recaptured my sweatshirt, so I was plenty warm enough.

We hadn't been out there more than ten minutes when I heard Dana's voice on the radio. I would have missed it if I hadn't stuck it into the pocket of my inside shirt. He simply said, "Trouble. At least one, maybe more."

I had my small revolver in the back waistband of my jeans, so I pulled it out. The deck had no stairs going off from it. Most likely, if anyone was headed into the house, it would either be through the kitchen door or a window. I walked down the hall to Gary's room. No surprise his bed was empty, and the pistol was gone. This wasn't all that good, because I didn't know the layout well enough to know where he would be.

It didn't take too long to find out. I had stepped into the room with the monitors in it when I heard a gunshot just outside of the bedroom I would be using.

The radio came to life and Gary's voice said, "One less."

I stayed where I was and waited, still with gun in hand. I was having a moment where I wondered if my heart rate would ever resume a normal rhythm again when Dana's voice came over the radio. "Two less."

I had not heard another shot, but I really didn't want to know. The monitor panel beeped. I stepped forward and looked at the screens. There was a man all dressed in black sneaking through the woods. I keyed the radio as Dana had shown me and as quietly as possible told him which screen it was on. All I got back was, "Roger that."

Whoever it had been was now out of sight on the monitor, so I could be of no more assistance. I was uncertain if Gary had heard the transmission, and I had no idea where he was.

Mercy had been standing with me in the room. Suddenly, she bolted out of the door toward the kitchen. She never made a sound, and when I rounded the corner, she was in the air sailing full tilt into a person dressed in black. The blessing here was the fact she had not announced her presence and had the advantage of surprise. He had a gun in his hand, and it discharged as she flattened him. I had my gun aimed directly at his head as he landed. Mercy was snarling with bared teeth while she stood on his chest.

"Don't move. Drop the gun or I'll blow your head off."

The gun clattered to the floor, but I didn't call her off because I was certain he had other weapons on him. The humorous thought running through my demented brain was I never have anything to tie these idiots up with. I should just shoot them and be done with it.

Thankfully, Gary came through the open door at that moment. He had relief written all over his face. He also had slip-ties in his pocket.

Dana ran up the walkway. Between the two of them, they made short work of disarming him and securing him.

We were steps away from the open door of the room with the monitors in it when I heard a 'beep.' "Dana, the monitor is beeping."

Dana stuck his head in the doorway and just said, "Shit, did they send the whole gang? There is another one on the path...gotta go now. Stay in the house."

Gary looked white as a sheet and about ready to fold. I dragged a chair over and pushed him down onto it. He put his head down between his knees as I prayed he wouldn't pass out and fall off.

We heard one single gunshot. Then nothing. Who shot whom was the question; I couldn't tell. I stood against the wall in the hallway next to the monitor room. We waited. Gary managed to sit back up. He still held his gun in his hand as did I.

This situation was way out of our control. How many more were there out there, and why?

Gary asked me to hand him the field phone off his nightstand. I was careful to stay against the wall and away from the windows while I retrieved it for him.

He took the phone and began speaking at once. "Need help now. Three invaders down, no idea how many more, at least one. Copy me."

Please, let someone hear him. We needed assistance badly. No one responded. I held my breath and prayed. I really and truly believed only God could help us.

Another beep from the monitor room. I looked inside and there on the screen was another man. I had no idea where Dana was because I didn't know anything about the placement of the cameras. I spoke softly into the radio, "Dana, another one on four."

Gary heard me and tried to get out of the chair. I pushed him back down gently and asked, "Where is four?"

"Under the deck. Get down and stay down. I'm going to slide out the door and see if I can get him."

"Like hell you are. Stay put. Right or left side?" I called Mercy to me and we slipped out the door. I knew she would know where the person was better than anybody.

I was correct. As dark as a pocket, she was right by my leg keeping me close to the building. Each time I took a step, I thought anyone on the mainland could hear me. We were almost to the corner of the building when Mercy stopped and backed into me, almost knocking me down. She froze then lowered herself into a crouch. I had my gun up and ready, but waited. Time was frozen. Suddenly, a bright light came on that was so startling I couldn't see anything. I dropped to the ground next to Mercy. Once I was below the beam, I could see it was someone with a hand-held spotlight. A shot rang out, and I saw the muzzle-blast from whoever was holding the light. All was quiet.

Dana called out, "Kate, are you okay."

"Yes, for the moment, I guess. Are you?"

"Am now."

Blessed be. Would this be the last one? Who knew? I had to go check on Gary. Mercy walked along beside me like we did this every day. I hoped this would be the last time in my life. I had been scared out of all of my nine lives and then some more I couldn't count. I am a person who does not even watch much television because I hate violence.

Gary was still in the chair and for some foolish reason, he was grinning. Either he had turned the mental corner, or he knew something I didn't. I didn't care...he was at least still alive.

I understood the grin when he spoke. "Coast Guard is sending a chopper and some men. They should be here within a half hour or so.

Don't be alarmed...they will set down on the big ledge. I already told Dana they were coming. That was why he had the spotlight. I'm so sorry to put you through this. I was certain we would have been safer here than any other place I knew."

The noise from the helicopter landing was unbelievable. Debris flew through the air like it was a hurricane. Then all was quiet. Until men began arriving at the kitchen door, I had no idea how many there were, and I didn't care. I was relieved.

There was a medic in the group and before they began checking the injured invaders, they checked Gary's wound. I was pleased to see his dressing was not soaked with blood.

The cottage was too full of people, and there were any number of conversations going on. I needed to retreat to a quiet spot and get my head back together. I carefully picked up Miss Joy and knew Mercy would follow along with me.

I walked into the kitchen on my way to the deck and, as I was passing the counter, I saw the glass of half-drunk wine I had poured before dinner. I picked it up, grabbed the box of wine, added some to the glass, and walked through the living room and out onto the darkened deck. I closed the door and shut out all of the multi conversations. Blessed peace.

It was dark on the deck, but with the reflected light shining from the interior of the house, we could see. It was getting cool, but with my sweatshirt on, I would be warm enough. I just wanted to stop the constant clamor going on in my head. It reminded me of trying to run too far at a fast pace. My body was out of reserves and needed a break to return to normal, whatever or whenever that might be.

As I sat there sipping my wine, a thought kept poking at me. This same thought had tried several times in the last few days to get my undivided attention. There had been too much mayhem creating stress so, although the idea surfaced, I had not been able to really pay attention. Now, it was out there, center stage and wanting to be recognized. Now, it was loud and clear: 'THIS WAS NOT ABOUT ME. IT WAS TOO BIG.'

I sat there, took a small sip of my wine and stared off into space. I had just had a mind-altering epic realization. I was not that important, nor did I wish to be. The who, what, and why these people were looking for, or trying to hide, had nothing to do with me. I was only an accidental inconvenience and nothing more. Talk about being in the wrong place at the wrong time.

Now that I had sorted this mess out in my head, I wanted out. Off this island and away from all the violence. I was going to go home and make sure my house was secure, load my camper and go camp, fish, kayak and relax with my two best friends, Mercy and Miss Joy.

My happy solution thoughts were rudely interrupted with the opening of the door and Gary rushing out onto the deck. "Thank God I found you, I had no idea where you had disappeared to. Why are you out here all by yourself?"

I just looked at this person. How could he ask such a stupid question? "Gary, I wasn't lost. You folks do not need me for anything else. I'm done with this craziness. As I told you in the beginning, this is bigger than anything to do with me. I don't know what it is about, but I do know it has nothing to do with me. I need to go home and get my life back. I hate violence on any level. This is for you and your folks to figure out. I'm done. Can you arrange for a boat or something to take me to shore so I can get my truck and be gone?"

He stood there like a statue made of stone and stared at me. Finally, he pulled one of the chairs closer and sat down. I could see he was struggling with an answer. "Kate, I can't let you go home until we get to the bottom of this and understand, as you mentioned, the who, what and why, of any of this. Did you miss any of what was happening here tonight?"

"No Gary, I was pretty involved, from my point of view. This is what I'm trying to explain to you. It's not me they're after. I'm not that important and never have been in my entire life. I just happened to be on the island and then here. I know you know some of what's going on and you won't share it with me. I'm good with not knowing, but I'm done with this whole mess. If you can't or won't, get me transportation back to the mainland, I'll contact someone to come out and pick us up. Right now, I'm going to bed. This has been a long day."

Gary extended his hand and touched my arm, "I'm sorrier than you are that you found yourself mixed up in this mess. If I really knew or understood all of what is going on, I would share it with you, even though I shouldn't. You came down here for a quiet vacation, and it has become a nightmare which won't quit. I feel as helpless as you do. It's not a feeling I deal well with. I came back to Maine after I retired. I was looking for the same things you came here for. I was enjoying my stay here on the island, doing some sailing and fishing, when they called me to investigate the murder on the island. It seemed odd to me they wanted or needed any expertise I had for something so simple. Truth be told, I was getting bored with retirement, so I agreed to do it."

My curiosity was engaged. "What did you do before retirement? Could this be something that followed you here?"

He shook his head. "I've pondered the same questions, but so far I haven't been able to connect the dots. I was in a special forces unit and investigated too many issues connected with, and to, international smuggling of arms, drugs, and human trafficking. I traveled the globe for years and have been involved in all kinds of crazy schemes.

"When I left the service, I was still young enough to be viable, with some interesting and questionable skill sets. I spoke several languages, possessed a good grasp of the differing regional dialects. I also had exceptional special ops training. I could fly almost anything and pilot a variety of watercraft.

"I was married for a short period of time. She divorced me, because according to her, I was too reckless to be husband material, let alone a parent. As I got older, and survived being shot, captured, plane wrecked to name a few, I agreed with her judgment of my character. I never anticipated ever getting anyone else in danger, least of all someone who is too innocent to warrant getting harmed."

I had listened to what he had to say. I was old, but not naïve. During my lifetime, I'd known someone almost with the same background. The blessing back then had been the problems were easier and not international. I was also young and madly in love. The issues still followed that person to our remote part of the map, and, from time to time, had to be dealt with. When the relationship ended, I was much more careful with whom I formed friendships. Fortunately, this was not a friendship, so I was free to leave and I intended to do exactly that in the morning, one way or another.

Gary had withdrawn his hand and was looking at me like Miss Joy sometimes does when she feels she needs a pat or a belly rub. I knew he didn't think he had made his case yet. When he spoke again, I was certain I wasn't going to be happy with the content.

I was right.

"I hope you know I would never let anyone harm you. I don't know you well, but I love the fact you're feisty and tough. I also don't know a lot about your background, but somewhere in your past, someone has roughed you up pretty good. I admire your guts and stick-to-it-attitude. In a fight, I certainly want you on my side. Please get some sleep and know we have some backup along with Dana to keep us safe."

My mind said, 'sure we do.' I would feel safe when I was back in my own space and not before. My only remark was, "Goodnight and get some rest. I'm sleeping with my pistol under the pillow, and Mercy guarding the room."

I was surprised at myself, because after a quick shower I fell asleep, and I don't think I even rolled over till it was dawn. I roused myself and went into the kitchen to make coffee. Once the carafe was full, I poured a cup and took the dogs out for a quick bathroom break before I fed them.

It was still cool outside and, in spite of all the battling last night, it was quiet and the air held the scent of the fir trees and the salty smell from the surrounding ocean. I love those smells...they always touch my soul. I could hear the bird songs along with the gulls. I walked the dogs out onto a point of land that dropped off to the shore below. It was a lovely craggy view. Very Downeast Maine.

Twelve

I took a sip of the coffee from the mug, and was just thanking God for the day when I was violently shoved off the ground. I didn't even have time to scream. I was busy trying to not get dashed to my death on the rocks. I had the good sense to try and protect my head.

I landed on a place where there was a small piece of earth covered with thick moss. I could, however, feel it was not very secure.

I wasn't able at the moment to determine if I was injured and if so, to what extent. I lay still and tried to catch my breath which had been knocked out of me when I hit the ground.

I needed to see if I could move at all. How had this happened? Where was Mercy? She never let anyone near me. Had somebody harmed her? I didn't have my revolver or my phone. I closed my eyes and took a deep breath to see if I could begin to determine the extent of my injuries. I couldn't feel anything, really. That was a very bad sign. I knew I was alive and breathing and I could see. My ears were ringing, so I knew from past accidents I had hit my head pretty hard.

I tried to move my arm; it hurt in the shoulder, but I could slide it along the ground. I tried the other arm and, although it was not as painful, I could move it. Next, I tried to move my foot. One of my feet felt colder than the other. Odd sensation. I needed to know why.

Had I broken my back again? I tried to move one of my legs. I thought I could move it some, but couldn't really feel enough to know.

Then the pain started. It radiated from the bottom of my feet to the last hair on my head. It came in waves, making my stomach want to heave. I passed out. When I came to, the pain was still there, and I had no idea of how long I had lain there. I needed help. I wasn't sure if I could yell or not, and if whoever shoved me heard me, would they come finish the job by pushing me over the edge to the rocks below? That would be certain death.

I didn't trust anyone. While I was trying to puzzle this part of the saga out, I passed out again. When I regained consciousness, I was aware of the fact I might have internal bleeding and could bleed out without anyone knowing. What a heck of a situation.

Something warm was breathing on me. I recognized the smell. Thank God, it was Mercy. I couldn't understand how she found me, but I needed her badly. She licked my face and I managed to open my eyes enough to see her. I tried to speak and it took me several attempts before I got the words out. "Mercy, go find Gary. Bring him to me. Go quick." That was the last thing I remembered.

I was getting fuzzy again when I heard someone speaking. I couldn't make out the words or the voice. I willed my mind with all my might to stay focused. When I opened my eyes again, Gary was there with Dana.

Gary was speaking, "I can't imagine how she fell off the banking or how she was lucky enough to land here and not on the rocks."

Had to tell them. "I didn't slip or fall, I was pushed."

"Kate, can you hear me? Where do you hurt? We need to get you up to the house. I just don't want to cause you any extra injuries or pain. How long have you been here?"

I knew my words would be limited, but I had to try. "Dawn. Don't know what is injured. You need to move me. I'm not much help at the moment."

Dana spoke up. "I can get the stretcher and pad we moved you with, but I need another person to carry her. You can't do it. Let me see if I can find Lou. I haven't seen him since last night after the chopper left. I'll be right back."

Mercy snuggled up next to my side; her warmth felt so good. Gary was kneeling beside me on the other side. He told me how he had found me. "Mercy came into my bedroom and nosed me awake, then began to pull my hand and wouldn't let go. I knew something was wrong, but couldn't understand what. I pulled on my clothes and she kept woofing at me. Once I slid my shoes on, she literally pushed me out through the door with her nose. She had my hand in her mouth pulling me down the trail when we met Dana. She stopped and barked at him, then began yanking on first my pantleg, then his. When we started following her, she began to run while looking back at us. I am so grateful for this dog. Please hang on for a few minutes more. Once we get you out of here, I'll call for a medical transport. Can you do that?"

I tried to nod, but it required too much effort. "No transport till I can assess my damages. Okay?"

Dana arrived with the stretcher and a man. Mercy stood and began to growl. This was a bad omen.

Gary was quick to figure out the situation and he directed Dana and the man how he wanted me loaded and carried. Mercy continued to growl and stayed by my head. When they tried to put me onto the stretcher, I passed out cold.

I became aware of my surroundings when they sat the stretcher on my bed.

I heard Gary speak to Dana. "I want you to lock him up until we check the cameras. This dog is never wrong. Do you understand what I'm saying?"

"I'll take care of it, Chief. Let me know if we need to take her ashore or need a Medi-vac."

In my lifetime, I'd been severely injured several times. I know that if I can get warm and figure out how badly I'm hurt, I can decide where I need to go. Home would be my first choice.

Already, the comforter Gary had placed over me was warming me. I was beginning to assess the extent of the personal damage. My medical staff was with me. Miss Joy was on the pillow by my head and Mercy was lying beside me, adding to the warmth. I don't know how she could be comfortable because she was half on the stretcher and the other half on the bed.

I began trying to move things again. I could get the right arm to lift. With a lot of effort, the left one moved a little. I tried to lift my head. I could, but only slightly. When I took a deep breath, my back hurt between the shoulder blades. I may have a fracture there. If so, it was a long painful process to heal it. I found out the reason one foot was colder than the other. I had lost a shoe. Dana had found it still sitting on the bank where I had been shoved off on my journey down the cliff.

I moved Mercy and pulled the comforter off so I could check my legs. I could move the right one slightly. I could also bend the knee some. The left leg was more resistant to movement, but I did get some motion and the knee would bend.

My main concern was my spine. I knew it would hurt like the dickens, but I had to try to roll onto my side. I opted to try to roll onto the side of the stretcher if I could. It took several tries before I succeeded with the help of hanging onto the edge of the stretcher. To say that hurt would be like comparing a puff of smoke to a volcanic eruption.

Once I got my breathing calmed down, I would try to roll the other way. That side took more effort and hurt even more, but I could manage it.

If I were going to be able to leave this place today and go home, I had to be able to stand and walk. For the moment, I couldn't even get off the damn stretcher below me. I would rest for a few minutes, then try to do more.

Gary was upset I wouldn't let him assist me. He got his courage up and came into the room with the offer to get me a cup of coffee. I relented and accepted the cup. He helped me put the other pillow under my head so I could sip without spilling.

He also had something else on his mind. "I checked the cameras and know what happened. It was Lou who pushed you off the bank. He was watching the house from the tree line. He waited until Mercy walked off the lawn to do her business, and then he made a dash for you. I don't know why, other than he thought we were together, and he wanted to get at me. I know nothing about him, but I will shortly. I am so sorry you are hurt. Have you determined what the injuries are yet? You must have a guardian angel who caught you and landed you on the only soft place on the cliff. There used to be a really nice spruce tree there until a hurricane a couple of years ago when it got ripped off, roots and all. What can I do to assist you?"

I needed to swallow my stubborn pride and see if, with Gary's help, I could stand or at least sit in a chair. "Gary, would you please give me a hand so I can see if I can stand or sit? First, we have to get this stretcher out from under me, or maybe just the pad."

Neither of us would be a good medic. I was injured and so was he. We settled on getting the pad off. By the time we had moved it out from under me, I was a wash of sweat and ready to heave. I took my time and rested until I felt I could at least try. The extensive bruising was not helping, because as time went by, they were getting really painful, and the muscles were tightening up. I was thankful I'd had on my heavy sweatshirt, so the abrasions were minimal.

What I wanted more than anything was some aspirin, a warm blanket and to sleep until the pain was gone.

Because of old injuries to my back, I knew I would have to swing around and get my feet on the floor from a sitting position on the bed, then try to stand. I managed to roll onto my side but lacked the strength in my arms to lift myself up to a sitting position and swing my legs off the bed. Damn. I hated being wimpy!

Gary understood what I was trying to do and put his good arm around my shoulders and lifted me, but when I tried to slide my legs off the bed, I couldn't get enough energy to do it. He assisted me to lie back down and roll over enough so he could tug the stretcher off the bed. I would need to take some aspirin and wait till later to try again.

Gary brought me the pills and water. I laid back and concentrated on getting warm. Mercy was like a large hot water bottle. I must have dozed off for a bit. When I woke, it took me a minute to figure out why I was in bed while the sun was up. My first attempt to roll over reminded me; it hurt like hell.

I was alone in the room with the dogs, so now was the time to try to get up. I rolled onto my side, grabbed the edge of the mattress for some leverage and tried to move my legs to the edge of the bed. I managed but was afraid to just slide my legs off the bed. If I had injured my lower back or spine, I could do a lot of damage.

I noticed the headboard of the bed was wrought iron. If I could slide myself up to it, I thought I could pull myself up. That would help. Once I got a grip on it, I used all my strength to try and sit upright. Okay, I knew I was making progress. Now, I needed to swing my legs over the edge. I kept my grip on the headboard for balance and willed myself to sit and see what would happen. I seemed to be stable. I was going to hang onto my handhold and try to stand. I prayed if I fell, I would land back onto the bed not the floor.

Mercy knew what I was trying to do, so she came around the bed and stood in front of me. Her expression said it all. She would help me, how I don't think either of us knew. I let go of the headboard and put my hand on the nightstand. It was sturdy; I would lean on that.

As I was sitting there trying to screw up my courage to attempt a stand, the thing running through my head was memories of an old accident. Years ago, before seat belts, I had been hit on the front-end by a car coming out of a crossroad going like a bat out of hell fleeing a police car. When he hit my car, I was catapulted out of the vehicle like a rag doll and rolled across the road and under his car. It happened so quickly I wasn't even frightened. The aftermath of the accident took weeks to get over.

I don't have weeks or even days. I needed to get up and out of here now.

With that thought in mind, I pushed and managed to get half up off the bed. It hurt. I wouldn't give in and sit back down. I had come this far. I could manage the pain. Thankfully, I have a high pain tolerance. If it killed me, I was going to stand. I did. Now, could I walk? I tried the first step while I steadied myself with the stand. I got to the door, but I was a wash of sweat from the effort. I breathed and leaned against the door jam. I would not return to the bed.

I couldn't hear anyone in the house and had no idea where everyone was. I had Mercy and Miss Joy with me. That was all I cared about. I stayed close to the wall in case I needed to balance myself. It looked warm and sunny outside. If I could get to the deck, perhaps the warmth and the sun would help revive me. I held onto the counter in the kitchen, getting almost to where I could step out onto the deck before Gary spotted me.

"What are you doing, Kate? Why didn't you call me to help? How on earth did you get upright? You're scaring the hell out of me."

He raced to my side and offered his arm for support. "Gary, I want to sit on the deck in the sun for a little while."

He was great support with his good arm. We looked like a couple of zombies. That was when Dana walked into the kitchen. He just stood there and shook his head. He laughed. "I can't leave the two of you alone for a second before you get into trouble. You guys are like naughty children." He opened the slider onto the deck and helped me onto the padded chaise lounge.

Once I caught my breath, the sun felt great. I still wasn't too sure what I had injured. I didn't care. I could stand and walk. I would be out of here shortly. I hoped I could drive my truck. It was going to take me some time at home to recuperate. I just needed to get there.

If things had been different, it would have been a great place to convalesce. I suddenly had food, a drink and potato chips and two men doting on me with both of my dogs sitting at attention, watching the chips.

Gary was the first to insist I needed to tell them what I wanted and where I hurt. The answer was easy. "I need to go home, and I hurt everywhere, which, I think, would be consistent after being shoved off a cliff."

I don't think it was the answer he was looking for. We all sat in silence. He knew I was serious about wanting to go. I knew he didn't want me to leave. What I didn't know or couldn't understand was why. Whatever was going on was way above my ability to process, grasp, or understand. I knew a small smattering of Gary's background from our conversation from the evening before.

Certainly, it was not enough to form any rational opinion about him or his life. Most likely, my questions ran to why he owned this island. Why was it set up with so much security? Why didn't he know more about the men he was affiliated with? Who was Dana, and why did he trusted him and no one else?

Gary was watching me with carefully concealed emotions, as was Dana. This was either okay or really bad. I couldn't read either of their faces. They must be crack poker players. This reminded me of an old-time movie...*The Standoff at the OK Corral.* I was becoming more uncomfortable by the nano-second. I hoped I could get off this chaise without embarrassing myself and do it alone, and with a modicum of dignity. I put my glass on the table next to the plate with the half-eaten sandwich and was ready to launch, or make a total idiot of myself in the process when Gary spoke.

"Kate, I know we're making you very uncomfortable. I can assure you it is not, and never has been, our intention to do that. I see you are processing what information you presently have about us and that you are wanting more information along with answers to your questions."

I reminded myself I had not voiced anything out loud. If they could read my mind, I wasn't going to wait for someone else to push me off the cliff; I was going to jump and get it over with on my own.

Gary nodded to Dana, then began, "I own this island because it's a birthright. It has been in my family since forever. We always used it as a summer place when I was a kid. Because it is on the outside away from the mainland, it had fortifications built on and in it during the second world war. Much like the island you grew up on. When the war was over, most of the sites remained intact because it wasn't necessary to remove them, and the family didn't care. When I would get tired of rambling around the globe, or needed a physical or mental rest, I would come and stay. After a particularly nasty incident, I added the security for peace of mind. Until now, I have never used or needed it. Does that ease your mind some?"

My goodness, he could even guess my thoughts. "Some, but not entirely. To be frank with both of you, I cannot understand, with your background, Gary, why you don't know more about the men you are associating with. Of all these people, and I mean no disrespect by asking, why do you have so much trust in Dana? Dana, why are you so devoted to Gary? I also would like to know why it is so important to either of you if I am here or gone? None of this has a darn thing to do with me. I am grateful for that, because I no long feel guilty about causing the fiasco on the other island. There. Now it's on the table."

Gary was the first to reply, "Great observation. We've been tracking drug and other illegal shipments in the area, but neither of us had any cause for concern about the island you were on. As far as we had ascertained, they were a bunch of old homeowners who hated strangers and no one ever went there. We left them alone. When I heard there was a suspicious death out there, it piqued my curiosity, so I sort of volunteered to check it out. Which, I might add, was a trigger for the local police department, setting off some of the concerns we saw as the result of when you were taken there.

"It was pure and simple a murder. The person was not a native, nor did anyone own up to knowing them. Mr. Peasley was sort of the island spokesman, and indicated you were the cause. Not for any reason, except you also were a stranger. It was the reason I came to see you. I knew you were not involved in any way, but still you were being threatened. Again, my cop's sixth sense. If the people who were doing it were not the natives, then who and why? After you found the corpse in the cave, I knew we were in too deep to walk away. Dana and I were led to believe the fishermen were running drugs. We knew it was not true because of the volume, and the network we were uncovering. We passed the mantle for this case on to a higher authority, but we became targets by the local police and their associates. This has been a very lucrative situation here for a long time. They don't want it to end, nor do they want to be convicted. Until it involved murder, they had gotten away clean."

I said, "None of this involved or continues to involve me, yet here I am...isolated, unable to return to my life, not to mention being shoved off a cliff. Why? Is this whole thing just for shits and grins, or is it going someplace? Don't you think I have a right to know?"

Dana had sat quietly while our conversations flowed. Now, he leaned forward in his chair. I couldn't read his eyes because he had a pair of really dark glasses on. His movements indicated he was ready to join the fray. "You do have very valid questions and I, for one, think you deserve some answers. I *am* devoted to Gary. You're absolutely one hundred percent correct on that observation. It's for a damn good reason. I've been Gary's 'wing man' for a long time. He saved my life years ago and nearly died while attempting my rescue. Anyone else would have run for cover instead of running into the line of fire coming from two sides. I'd been shot so many times I didn't think another breath was possible. Yet, here's this guy I'd never seen before dragging me by the feet off the firing range. He was also a fairly good field medic. How he kept me from bleeding out, I'll never know. When I came to in surgery, he was on the next table giving me his blood to keep me alive. And by the way, I am with the Drug Enforcement Agency and have been for years. I have also done a stint with Interpol on drug and other issues. We had never met before that day."

Gary looked a little embarrassed at Dana's disclosure. "We've worked closely together ever since. We understand how each of us thinks, which is a bonus when things get dicey. Dana is to me what Mercy is to you. He senses things I might have overlooked or passed on. He has saved my bacon plenty of times. We had been checking out several leads in the past couple of days, and they resulted in several folks in the local police and Coast Guard being removed from their posts. Until this thing happened, even though folks knew I had been service-related, they didn't connect me with the raids or the monitoring of the boats offshore. They just have always assumed Dana was my sidekick and of no concern to them. We changed the play card when we got involved with rescuing you from the island and then removing you from their custody in the manner we did. Now, we are targets along with you."

He continued on. "My thinking is for you to stay a couple of days until we determine the extent of your injuries and you get healed, so you are at least mobile. Then we will get you home. Do you think you can tolerate us for a couple more days?"

I nodded and was truthfully wondering if I was going to even be able to get off the chaise I was sprawled on without a Hoya lift. "How closely are we being watched, do you know? What interest would anyone have in me? Why would they blow their cover to harass me?"

Gary looked at Dana, then with a grim expression on his face, spoke carefully. "Kate, we did some research on you. Please don't be offended, but something wasn't adding up. We know you owned and operated a small business for many years and dealt with fishing boats and other unrelated businesses. During the last few years, you worked with a number of boats from a port in Massachusetts and their crews. There were some issues with at least one of those boats. It was kept pretty quiet, but that whole crew ended up being prosecuted and getting substantial prison time. Lou, the man who shoved you off the banking, was the son of the captain on the boat. His father died in jail. Old grudges die hard. I don't think he sought you out, but when the opportunity presented itself, he acted. We would like you to stay here while we see if anything else surfaces. Can we agree on at least a resting time for a couple of days?"

I was shocked with the news. I had started, developed, and run my business for several years, and because of the nature of what I did, it hadn't been unusual to encounter some fraudulent cases requiring my testimony or records to prove a case. Most were resolved by my bringing the problem to the owners and letting them deal with the issues. At the end of owning the business, the cases were getting more involved while requiring extensive investigations to make litigation successful. I had enjoyed the business when it began because I dealt mostly with individuals who owned commercial fishing boats or small businesses. Back then, other than the crew trying to hide a little extra shack money for the trash fish onboard, life was easy and everyone was happy.

Finally, a man who rented office space from me wanted to buy me out. I was happy with the price and a promise of freedom from a seven day a week commitment, so I sold. I moved on with my life and honestly had never looked back.

I could see Gary was expecting me to at least reply beyond the nodding of my head. "I'm shocked but appreciate your effort to tie it together. I'm willing to stay for a few days and determine my physical damages, then you'll be rid of one more issue."

I had an afterthought. "Did you ever identify either of the two folks murdered on the island or why they were killed."

Dana answered. "Not entirely, we're still working on it. I have a feeling they may be involved with something we didn't even know about, or suspect. Not a very comprehensive answer to your inquiry but, at the moment, it's all I have."

I am never going to elaborate on how, or what, it took to get me standing and erect because it embarrasses me to even think about it. Let's just say I was grateful for the assistance.

I lounged around for another day before I tried a walk with the dogs. It was tough going, but I could manage it if I rested and didn't try to go too far. Thankfully, the island was peaceful and quiet. I rested and spent lots of time on the deck in the sun. On my last day there, I walked down the path about halfway to the shore. I struggled to hike back up to the cottage, but once I made it, I was sure I was okay and ready to go home.

In the evening at dinner, we discussed my leaving the next day. Gary didn't look as if he thought it was a good idea, and Dana stayed silent. There hadn't been any issues on the property that I knew about. I was restless and ready to get home. Other than what I was certain was perhaps a fractured disk between my shoulder blades, I had no other broken bones and the rest of the body seemed as good as ever, except with the bruising and lameness. I had broken my back in the same place years before in another auto accident. A man had rear-ended my car. I was just concerned about what my husband was going to say about the damage to the auto. As a side note, he was delighted the car was totaled; he never asked if I was injured. At the time, I was too naïve to know what had happened to my body. It takes a long time to heal and stop hurting, but there isn't anything you can do except let nature take its course.

We agreed the next day they would take me to the landing where my truck was parked. Dana was in favor of doing it after dark in case someone was watching the vehicle. He was planning to go in during the day with a small skiff and check everything out. Gary would then take me over in the evening. I was fine with the precautions. I didn't want or need any more problems.

I got everything packed and late in the day we made our way down to the boat with the ATV and the cart. The dogs were both happy to go on any adventure. I wished for the thousandth time I had half their energy and enthusiasm. Truth be told, I think Gary was ready to be off the island, too. He had his arm out of the sling, even though it was tender at the end of the day.

Unlike some folks, I enjoy being on a boat at night and just sailing along watching the stars and the glow of the phosphorus kicked up from the prop wash. I think I would have made a great sailor.

As we neared the mainland, Gary got a call from Dana about where we would meet. Dana had taken an extra precaution and moved my truck. He had taken it to a shopping center and parked it for a while. He reported no issues, so they decided on the town float. I didn't care where it was. I just wanted to be in my own vehicle, alone and with the dogs. Gary and Dana had been good company and had allowed me my space, but I've lived alone for years, so I am most comfortable when I'm on my own.

We docked at the float where Dana met us. He carried my stuff to the truck while Gary and I said goodbye. Gary was hesitant to release me when he hugged me. I was ready to be gone. He was a nice person, but I didn't need anyone else in my life. When he let his arm drop off my shoulder, he said, "Please call me and consider coming back for a visit when things are not so chaotic. I would really enjoy having you and the dogs."

I smiled, "Thanks Gary, you have been a great support during all this mess. I appreciate the time and energy you've devoted to us. I still have your card and, if I get into another jam, you would be the first person I'd call. How's that for an answer."

I knew it was a smart-aleck way to get around the invitation, so I just smirked and kept my mouth shut. Least said, easiest mended. All my life I'd left situations when they were finished without ties. I wasn't going to begin a new pattern at this age.

Dana was standing by the truck with the door open waiting for us when I walked up the ramp. I told the dogs to load up, then turned and said, "Thanks, Dana, I appreciate the fact you took the extra time and effort. It has been a pleasure to know you. Take good care of Gary, he seemed kind of sad. I'm sure his mood will change as soon as you two get involved in another adventure." We shook hands and I hopped into my truck.

Thirteen

The drive home was what I always imagined a pilgrimage would be like. I was full of anticipation with a slight edge of dread. I had been away from my home for a long period of time. Leaving property empty is never a good idea, even when the weather is warm. I rationalized it with the thought 'it would be, what it would be.' I'd deal with it tomorrow. Tonight, I just wanted to sleep in my own bed.

The first thing in the morning, as I was making coffee, my cell phone rang. It was Gary.

"Was everything okay when you got home? Are you feeling all right? Are the dogs happy to be home?" He sounded anxious; I wondered why. By his own admission, the man had been a loner and a rolling stone all his life.

"Good morning, Gary, we are all fine. I haven't had much time to survey the surroundings. I'm certain everything will be as I left it. I hope you and Dana have a good day and enjoy some quiet time spent without babysitting duties."

It was clear he was not ready to end the call. "Kate, the island seems empty without you and the dogs. I do hope you'll plan on coming back soon. I hope you understand you are *always* welcome. Just give me a call and I'll be at the dock waiting for you."

I needed to nip this in the bud. "Thank you for the invite. I'm planning to take a trip up north with the camper for some fishing before it gets too much later in the season. There isn't much, if any, cell coverage up there, so you most likely won't hear from me anytime soon. Thank you and Dana for all your assistance and the hospitality. Now that you are not babysitting, go sailing and do some fishing. You two could use some fun. Say hello to Dana for me, please."

"Kate, will you promise to call me when you get back from your camping trip?"

"I will, and thank you again. Have a good day. Bye for now." I disconnected the call, or it would have gone on throughout my breakfast. I didn't want to give him any false signals of interest on my part. I'm not a very trusting person, and, for some reason or other, I had the feeling there was still unfinished business with him. I was truly done, but somehow, I had the nagging sense there was still something else going on I had no clue about.

I puttered around the house checking things out. Everything seemed to be in order, with the exception of my gardens. The flower beds were in desperate need of weeding, and the vegetable beds were overrun with ripe and overly ripe produce. I considered weeding for about twenty seconds, then decided to salvage what I could of the veggies.

After a fast laundry job, I packed the camper and we were ready to head out for a camping trip in a quiet and remote spot in the northern regions of our state. It had once been owned by the paper companies and now was state land for recreational uses. As often as I had been there camping, I had only seen a very few folks. It was not a place where people go to socialize; they went there to fish, hunt, and hike in blessed solitude.

As always, the dogs were all excited about going anywhere. This was going to be Mercy's first trip in the camper, other than the ride to the vet's office the first day when I had saved her. What a dog! I loaded our stuff, then called the dogs. Miss Joy made her way up the steps and into the rig while Mercy sat on the grass waiting for her turn. Once Miss Joy cleared the top step, Mercy made one bound and landed inside. Boy, I wished I could do that. Those days of 'bounding' were over for me.

I had packed my fishing rods. I had fly, spinning and jigging equipment. I always carry an inflatable kayak. I hoped the three of us would not swamp it. If so, we all knew how to swim. It would be just another part of our *new* adventure.

I put the electric steps up, closed and locked the camper side door. I walked around to the driver's side and stepped up into the rig. I could see the seating order had already been established. Mercy sat in the passenger seat and Miss Joy was sitting on the hassock I'd placed between the seats for her years before. We were good to go. It was comforting to have just me and the dogs. Now, I was in charge of any plans or changes I wished, or wanted, to make.

Our drive north was without incident. We stopped for a sandwich break and a short pee time for the dogs, then we were off again. I like to get to the site late in the afternoon so I can get set up and have time to enjoy the sunset, a glass of wine, and early evening.

When we arrived, there was one other camper already in place. They were parked at the far end of the allotted space. I could see they also had a boat trailer, so most likely they were still out on the water. I didn't see or hear a dog. I put out our mat, chairs, table, and opened the awning. The weather was perfect. I pulled out the kayak and began the task of inflating it with the foot pump. It takes me a while to do, but it isn't a terrible job. Mercy was curious, but Miss Joy knew exactly what I was doing.

I decided we still had enough daylight to give the kayak a short trial with the three of us onboard. After all, it was still warm enough, if we ended up swimming. I carried it down to the shore. The beach there is sandy with no rocks. Perfect for launching an inflatable. When I bought the boat, it had come with a wooden floor. I had never seen one but thought it a great idea with dogs and sharp claws. I'd only had Miss Joy then; now I have a big dog. *I'll see how this plays out.* Both dogs sat on the floor and watched the process of my boarding and getting us afloat. Neither moved. What great gals.

We paddled along the shoreline for a short distance then went in to prep our dinner, have a glass of wine and enjoy the sunset. Best of all was the blessed alone time with peace and quiet.

A little after sunset, I heard a boat motor heading for the shore. It sounded like a trolling motor. Our neighbors must be returning from their fishing and boating trip. They came ashore, nodded in our direction and walked on to their rig. Later, I could smell fish cooking on the soft evening breeze. Paradise at last. We took a small stroll, then returned to get ready for bed.

It was a pleasant evening with very moderate temps and a soft breeze, so I left our windows open. We all piled onto the bed, which is the sofa folded down. I'm too claustrophobic to sleep in the bunk over the cab. My excuse is the dogs couldn't get up there, and the truth is neither can I easily, especially now.

I have owned many campers over the years, both large and small. Some brand new, others used. When I bought this, I wanted a small one. At twenty-one feet, it was perfect. It was older but had been well maintained by the original older couple who had bought it new. They had carefully cared for it and, at their age, had treated it nicely. It was perfect for the wilderness camping I wanted to do with plenty of space for me and the dogs.

Early morning came with a beautiful sunrise. I put the coffee on to perk, took the dogs for the mandatory stroll for pees and other necessities. We returned for breakfast while the sun rose and warmed the camper. The air was so fresh it was a treat to smell the forest and the lake. Every day should begin like this.

I was just deciding what type of fishing I was going to attempt when our neighbor began readying his boat to put it onto the trailer. We would wait until they left to go fishing. I wasn't in any hurry to do anything except relax.

Once the other folks left the parking area, we had it all to ourselves, so I allowed the dogs to be loose. We got into our boat and went off to explore the shoreline. I hadn't been into this campsite for over a year and just wanted to re-familiarize myself with the topography.

I had packed us a snack with some drinks so we could stay out on the water for quite a period of time if we choose to. I decided to try my luck with fishing while we were in a small cove. I remembered I had caught some nice trout the last time I was there. The beauty of the inflatable is it's so quiet I don't think fish even know we are hunting them. It wasn't long until we had our first nibble. Dinner was on the way. I'd brought a small bucket just in case I caught anything. I slipped the fish off the hook, rebaited, and put it back out. When I had another fish, I stopped fishing and paddled for shore. Why take too many when I had a whole lake full of fish out there? Tomorrow would be another day and, if so, they would be one day larger.

We went for a walk down the road and back, prepped for dinner and poured a glass of wine. The timing was perfect. The sun was low across the water, making the sky a photographer's dream. I got my large camera out and snapped some photos. Years ago, I would have taken more shots, developed the film in my small darkroom and printed only the ones I wanted. Digital was a much easier gig, giving good quality results. This was perfect. Life doesn't get any better than this, ever.

The weather held perfect for the next couple of days. No other folks showed up to use the camping area, so we enjoyed the whole space.

On the third day, we went hiking in the woods on what looked to be a rough trail. I had sprayed for ticks and taken all the precautions before we set off. Even though we were the only ones in the lot, I still locked the camper when we would go off. I also always carried my revolver. This area is well known for its black bear population. I've never been bothered by any of the wildlife. I did wake up one morning years ago to find a small black bear sleeping on my mat outside of the door. I have also watched a moose walk through the camping area. I always gave them a wide berth, especially when it is mating season. They are extremely large animals and can be dangerous during a rut.

We saw a doe with her fawn who was almost the same size as the mother. We crossed an open field of sorts and kicked up some partridge. I needed to remember this spot for fall camping and bird hunting. Thankfully, my life was coming back into perspective.

I no longer hunt deer. That revelation came to me several years earlier while I was hunting five miles from my truck and, as always, was alone, when I spotted a nice buck. Just before I pulled the trigger, my mind engaged and I recalled all those facts. I was alone and five miles through the woods from the vehicle. I made a deal with myself: unless the deer would come, lie on my fender, or get into the back of the truck, then let me shoot it, I was done. Besides all those factors, I don't eat much meat. I love to bird hunt. They are easy to carry and I love eating them.

We wandered back to the camper and enjoyed a lazy late afternoon, just sitting and relaxing while reading. I was pouring a glass of wine and making a munchie tray when I heard a rig coming up the road. I called the dogs in and prepared to leash them.

The rig came into the lot, made a U-turn and drove off, back down the road. Great, peace had returned to our space. I hadn't even noticed if they were from out-of-state. I also didn't really care. There are several of these wilderness campsites, and I knew if you stayed on the main road coming in, it also branched off to another site on a different small pond further up the road. I had been coming here for many years back when it had been owned by the paper company.

Fourteen

That evening, we had some cloud cover and the breeze increased, so we didn't sit out too long. I was tired, so we got ready for bed early. It was cooler, so I wore my sweats to bed. We had been in bed for a couple of hours when Mercy began to growl. It was her soft low sound. I was surprised, because all the time we had been there she hadn't made a sound other than her play noises. Once she started, Miss Joy became restless as well.

I hadn't heard anything unusual, but I had also been sound asleep. I listened, not hearing anything but the wind in the trees. I had the jacklight sitting on the floor beside the bed, in case I needed it. I kind of dismissed the whole thing and rolled over to go back to sleep, when Mercy reached out her paw and touched me. Sometimes she does that when she needs to get my attention. Perhaps she needed a potty break.

I began to get out from under the covers. She laid on top of me, pushing me back down onto the sofa. This was becoming too reminiscent of the situation on the island. I began to listen intently and fished the revolver out of the pocket of my jacket. There was no way I could drive off. I had the chairs and mat out, as well as the steps and awning. Our kayak was slid under the rear of the camper so the wind wouldn't blow it away. I sent a silent prayer up, *'please God not another situation.'* Maybe she had heard an animal. Although we had seen deer today and yesterday and watched a small black bear walk across the road, she hadn't made a sound. I knew she had seen them because when we got to the place where the bear crossed, she'd sniffed the tracks.

Well, perhaps the folks who had driven in before had decided to come back. I hadn't heard a vehicle, though.

It was almost dawn, so I just stayed in bed and waited until there would be sufficient daylight to check things out. Mercy was silent while we lay there, even though she was almost on top of me. Perhaps whatever she heard had moved off and was no longer on her 'threat' list.

Daylight finally came and, although it was still overcast, it was not raining. When I opened the door to take the dogs out, I noticed it must have rained a bit during the early evening. I was about to step down off the step when I noticed at the edge of our mat there were footprints in the dirt. I was alarmed because I could see whoever they belonged to had come out of the woods behind us and walked around our camper, then back into the woods. Why would anyone be out at night walking around in the woods? Let alone make a pass through the campground? My wary meter came on full tilt.

I put my revolver into my sweatshirt pocket and took the dogs for their business walk. A very short one. We stayed in sight of the camper. I wasn't sure what I wanted to do about this development. I hate folks who get all paranoid over small things. I needed to decide if this was a small thing.

The sun was not out and the wind was gusting pretty strong, so I knew we wouldn't be going out with the boat or fishing. Perhaps the weather would clear up later in the day.

We had a nice breakfast and I curled up with a new book after the dishes were done. About noon the sky began to clear and the wind dropped to just a slight breeze. It had also warmed up nicely. I opened the windows in the camper and we sat outside for a short time. I really wanted to go out with the boat and fish for dinner. Both of the dogs were calm and I didn't sense any issues. The footprints still bothered me; however, I was determined not to let something like that spoil our trip. I had planned on staying at least three more days before heading home.

I locked up the camper, took the dogs and the boat down to the shore. We were just getting ready to get into the boat when Mercy began her low growl again. It was louder than it had been last night. She was staring intently at the camper. I pulled the kayak up onto the bank and began walking back toward the camper. Mercy was a few steps ahead of me and her eyes were laser focused on a spot just to the left of our site. I followed her sightline but couldn't see anything unusual. I trusted her. Something was going on over there, even if I couldn't spot it. She was all blocked up and intent on whatever she had seen.

By the time we reached the camper, she had settled down somewhat, was no longer growling, and her posture had softened. I was done with this game. I took Miss Joy to the camper and put her inside out of harm's way.

Mercy and I walked into the woods to see what was going on. She walked just a couple of steps ahead of me, then stopped. I could see the forest floor was all scuffed up and guessed it had been an animal she had seen. I was ready to go back and finish our fishing trip. I turned to leave the spot and she stepped in front of me. Clearly, she was not ready to leave. I watched her sniff the ground and walk on a few more steps where she stopped and looked at me. What was she trying to show me? I stepped forward and realized she was looking at footprints made by a man, or a damn big woman. Whoever they were, they had also field dressed a cigarette and tried to scuff dirt over the remains. It looked like a single set of prints.

Now my quandary was: should I follow the trail someone had left behind, or go move our camper to avoid any issues? I had just dealt with enough situations to last a lifetime and was not looking to re-engage with anyone else...now or ever.

It was getting late in the afternoon. If I broke camp now, I wasn't sure where we would go to find another spot for the night. Or for that matter, a couple more days. I knew I needed to begin to close up camp even if I stayed for the night. We walked back to our site and I began mentally organizing the closing.

My first priority was to retrieve the kayak from the shore. Mercy walked with me in lockstep down to the shore and back. I could tell she was guarding by the expression on her face and the stance of her walk.

It didn't take us long to get everything packed away. My heart was heavy; I wasn't anywhere near ready to leave. I decided I wouldn't deflate the kayak, just in case this whole thing would have some logical explanation and we could stay. I again slid it under the rear of the camper so it wouldn't blow away if we got any wind.

I fixed some dinner but forewent the usual glass of wine. I needed to be alert if we had to leave quickly. The problem with leaving after dark was the road was narrow and rutted in places. I could get blocked in easily if someone wanted to stop me.

I was sitting, watching the gathering dusk, when a dark thought occurred to me: was this some of Gary's doing? If so. I would drive a stake in it. I was not going to be imprisoned by any more of his foolishness. I grabbed my cell and stepped outside the camper. I knew I had coverage in that spot because I'd checked it once before today just in case I needed it.

Fifteen

I punched in his number and could hear it ringing. On the second ring he answered with a heartfelt greeting, "Hi there, how are you? This is a really pleasant surprise to hear from you. Where are you? Is everything okay?"

My turn. "Obviously everything is not okay, or I wouldn't be calling you. Do you have someone trailing me? If so, why?"

A stunned silence followed. "Kate, I don't have any reason to have someone follow you, and I wouldn't do so without telling you and who it would be. Where are you, and what's going on? Now I'm concerned because I'm still on the island and so is Dana. How far away are you?"

Moment of truth...could I trust him? I was out of options. "I'm camping on state land above Route Nine. Someone walked around the camper last night and today I found a fresh place where they had been in the woods behind the campsite. They were there long enough so they'd smoked a cigarette and expended enough energy to field dress the butt. There isn't anyone else here at this campsite. There was another camper when I came, but they pulled out early the next morning. The next day, a camper pulled in, made a U-turn and left without stopping. In itself, that wouldn't have been odd, because most folks who camp here prefer to have the space all to themselves."

I could hear Gary's intake of breath on the other end of the line. His response was immediate. "I *am* being honest with you. I do not have anyone following or looking for you. I don't like the sound of this. If I call a warden or the state police, could they find you? It would take us too long to get there to be effective. Are you armed?"

I sighed. "Of course I'm armed, but I only have my .38 with me. I was only planning on camping, fishing, and a bit of hiking. I am concerned about calling the wardens or other law enforcement because they'll think I'm a certifiable old lady nutcase. I'm also reluctant to pull out at this time of day because it's over an hour on a very rutted, narrow road. If I got blocked in, I would be unable to back away or take another road. Whoever is watching me can't be too far away. The next area for a campsite is back down the road, and then off on a fork going north. It has to be over five miles through the woods and closer to eight on the road."

The next question surprised me. "Is there enough room on the lot to land a small chopper?"

I didn't know how to answer that one. "I would think so. There is enough space for a fairly large rig to make a swing around, then pull out. The campsites are back against the trees with a pretty large open area between them and the lake."

"Kate, do you know the coordinates for the campground?"

I thought for a moment. "I have the *Maine Gazetteer* with me. Why?"

Gary chuckled. "Can you give me the references from that? If I lose you, call me right back."

I ran into the camper and grabbed the book. I hoped I could be accurate with how I read it. I gave Gary the best references I could. I also knew it would be too dark for any flight this late in the day. My afterthought was how had it come down to looking to him for assistance. I was about ready to cancel any plans he might have hatched when Mercy began to growl in earnest. "Gary, I have to go. Mercy is getting really serious here, and I need to be paying attention to what's going on."

Gary shouted, "Kate, leave the phone open and take cover if you can. We're on our way!"

I reached into my pocket to be certain I had the revolver. I only ever keep five bullets in it and rest it on an empty cylinder. I needed to get some ammo into my pocket. With that thought in mind, I dashed into the camper and dumped a handful of bullets into my sweatshirt pocket.

I didn't want to be trapped in the camper if someone was sneaking around, but I couldn't take a chance on Miss Joy getting harmed either. I needed her to be inside and silent. Never an easy task, because she always wanted to be with me and Mercy. I set her dinner down, hoping to distract her, and praying she would hop up onto the sofa and take a nap after she ate. From the way Mercy was acting, I didn't have the luxury of time to figure anything else out. I needed to get outside now and be hidden to be somewhat effective.

We slid out through the door and moved slowly to the small cluster of scrub trees which sort of separated the lots. Thankfully, Miss Joy was not barking. The dusk was rapidly turning to darkness. I hadn't grabbed the jacklight. I did have my phone. If we had to sit out here all night in the cool and dark in order to make it through to dawn, I was mentally prepared to do it. For the hundredth time, I asked myself *why?* What was it that prevented me from just going off and enjoying a vacation like everyone else without any drama?

Mercy and I settled on an old fallen log to wait. Wait for what, I hadn't a clue. I wished I had brought the light with me, but it was too late to go back and get it without giving us away. It was also cooler than I had anticipated, so it wasn't long until I was not only mentally bemoaning the missing light, I added a jacket to the list, and a nice thermos of hot tea. I wouldn't ever make a great night fighter. I get too easily bored and I become very restless. On the other hand, Mercy was sitting beside me with her body against my leg as if to reassure me it would be okay.

I ran my memory banks, trying to reason out why anyone would be here bothering me. I tried to remember all the people I had worked with to see if I had forgotten something. After being pushed off the bank by Lou, I was concerned. Soul searching is not my strong suit. I thought I had always been fair and kind in my dealings with people. When something came up that was criminal in nature, and I had been called on for a reference or as a witness, I had been honest, but never mean-spirited. I couldn't think of anything, so we just waited and shivered.

It is amazing how you can go from being close to frozen in place and ready to quit, to being energized and way too warm when a branch snaps off to your left. While we had been sitting there, I had heard small animals scurry behind us and neither Mercy nor I had paid any attention. Now, we were both intently alert, although she was silent. I knew from her posture she was ready for whatever. I had the revolver in my hand. I didn't need to check and see if I was ready. When threatened, I am *always* ready. That is the advantage of growing up alone on the streets as a kid. A trait of priceless value that you, thankfully, never lose.

Another branch snapped, this one closer to us. I watched in the direction the sound came from while keeping Mercy's head in my line of vision. The blessing, if there was one, was that even without a moon, the stars' reflection on the lake, and the fact our vision had adjusted during darkness falling assisted in my ability to see movement. Nothing yet. Be patient. Something or someone was there; I could feel it to the base of my being.

Whoever was in the woods didn't hurry, waiting for long periods of time before advancing. We waited. The hunter and the hunted. I was unsure which role we were playing or why. Another snap. Much closer now. Mercy rumbled but didn't growl aloud. I relaxed I was beginning to get the rhythm of the game now. I could wait.

Apparently, whoever was there wanted something that was important enough to them to play out the time frame necessary to gain the prize. What the prize was, I hadn't a clue. When we got to the final act, I would have the answer. I have always been more interested in the why than the what.

This time, the wait was the longest one yet, but it came with a very distinct snap which I gauged was no more than twenty feet from where we were sitting. Mercy turned her head to look at me and leaned back strongly against my leg as if to caution me. I nudged her back as an acknowledgment. We continued to wait. I kept mentally thanking God for the gift of Mercy.

I had no sense of how long we had been at the game. I knew the end was near, one way or the other. Whoever it was would make a critical move shortly. I could feel the tension in the air. They were very close. I could also smell tobacco smoke faintly on the breeze, as it wafted by us. I knew Mercy had smelled it, also.

Another snap. This one was close and in front of us. I was hoping I could get a silhouette against the backdrop of the lake. I waited. At last, I was rewarded for my patience. The person took one more step, and I could clearly see it was a man and he held a gun in his hand. The dumb fool had a stainless-steel gun, and it showed up clearly.

He crouched down and began to sidle to the camper door. He held the gun in his right hand and was perhaps eight feet from the camper when I stood. We had selected our spot very carefully, so it was all grass and pine needles. We moved silently behind him and outside his peripheral line of sight. I knew where Mercy was, because she was just brushing my leg as we moved. It seemed like it was a mile or more to travel just to get within a reasonable distance of him.

My camper is white and he was in perfect relief against it. I didn't want to startle him and have him take a shot at us. We were too close for him to miss. I also didn't want to shoot a hole in the camper, if I could help it. He stood as if listening for some sound from within the unit. I was surprised, because with all of his stealth, he hadn't sensed our presence behind him. He was so focused on what he thought was going to be an easy invasion he was not using the same caution he had been for getting there.

From his posture, I knew he was going to take a step forward, and when he stepped, so did I. He never heard us. He decided to change hands with his gun, and I instantly recognized my opportunity to make a move. I stepped directly behind him and jammed my gun into the small of his back. "Don't move. Don't breathe or you're dead. Drop the gun. Now!"

He hesitated for a half a second, then began to lift his forearm. Before he could get the arm raised any higher, Mercy had her teeth sunk into his arm to the bone. The gun fell and he screamed.

"Back up slowly or the next thing she will rip out is your throat and I won't call her off."

He carefully stepped back. I could see he was looking around wildly as if trying to figure out how far or fast he could run to get away from us. Mercy hadn't let go of his arm. He was semi-dragging her along as he was backing up. I could see his gun lying on the ground where he had dropped it. I wasn't going to break my concentration in order to pick it up. Without a mighty lunge on his part, he couldn't reach it either.

I had him. Actually, Mercy had him. Now I needed to secure him. Same old problem I keep having. No damned rope! I reached into my storage bin under the camper and pulled out one of the rachet ties I carry with me at all times. Second problem…what to attach him to for safe keeping. I opted for the spare tire on the back of my rig.

When I was done, it wasn't pretty or necessarily neat, but he was trussed from top to bottom with two sets and ratcheted so tight he could scarcely breathe. Like I could care.

Other than to scream, he had not said a word. He was terrified of Mercy and I had no intention of changing his mind. I had picked up his gun. It was a 357 Ruger revolver with a long barrel.

I had stopped to catch my breath and was praying I would not get the shakes, when my cell phone rang and I nearly jumped out of my skin. It was Gary. "Kate, are you okay? We aren't too far away. Can you turn on the headlights of the camper so I can spot you?"

"I can. Do you need me to move the rig so it will light the ground where you need to land?" I ran to the cab and pulled on the light switch.

His answer was swift. "No, I have landing lights. I just need to find you in this forest. Be there shortly."

I had just enough time to stick the phone back into my pocket when I heard the blades of the chopper. I was surprised. He definitely didn't need my lights to land. He could illuminate a football field with his. The flying dirt and debris were terrible. I was afraid we would get either hit with a stone or impaled on the sticks. Thankfully, it only lasted a minute.

Gary was the first one out, while Dana was busy with whatever needed to be done to stop the machine. He ran around the bird and headed straight for me until he spotted the body strapped to the spare tire. He walked to the rear of the rig. That was where Dana caught up with him at the same moment. They both looked, then burst into laughter. I thought they were going to pass out from lack of air they were laughing so hard. I walked over to them and just stood looking at the idiots. Had they never seen a person restrained?

Sixteen

Dana had a small flashlight he shone on the face of the person I had captured. Dana was the first to stop laughing, and he sobered immediately. Gary followed suit and took a good look at the man, shaking his head. Suddenly, both of the men were sober-faced and serious as a heart attack.

Gary walked over to me and asked, "Who did he say he was? Did he tell you why he was sneaking around your site?"

"Nope, he hasn't uttered a word other than to scream bloody murder when Mercy bit his arm. I wouldn't make her let go until I had him secured. His gun is on the step of the camper."

"Kate, this is real bad news."

I was certain Gary was going to tell me I had either a warden or a law enforcement person strapped to my spare tire. Now, I was really going to be in deep trouble. Well, I might as well know now as to worry about something I had no control over. "What is the problem, Gary? Is he law enforcement? State or Federal?"

"Kate, take a deep breath. He is neither. The Feds have been searching high and low for this guy for weeks. He has a hell of a bounty on his hide, dead or alive. I can't believe you managed to capture him without getting hurt, or worse, killed. He is wanted for breaking out of prison. He killed two officers and another inmate in the break. They suspect he is to blame for a couple of random murders, since he has been on the run as well. He was being held for a mass murder spree out in the Midwest. My knowing you is going to give me heart failure for certain."

Dana walked up and smacked me on the back, then gave me a hug. "Well kiddo, you really did it this time. There will be enough police here shortly and commotion so they will never allow you to camp here again. Gary, just to be on the safe side, I'm going to sit there and watch him with my pistol in hand. I think Mercy plans on standing guard also."

I decided there were enough of them I didn't need to be involved any longer. I went into the camper and made a pot of coffee. I was exhausted. It had been a damn long night, and dawn was beginning to break at the edge of the sky. Perhaps now I could stay for another couple of nights, rest up, and do some fishing. Well, I always was a dreamer, along with being an eternal optimist.

In a matter of a couple of hours, the camp's lot was full of cars, trucks, and people. Some in uniforms, some not, but all flashing badges. It seemed as though they were all talking at once and asking the same questions over and over. I locked the camper, took Miss Joy and Mercy and walked down to the other end of the lot for some quiet. We were sitting on a large flat boulder at the water's edge when Gary found us.

He was trying to be casual when he asked, "Is this seat taken or is it open to the public?"

I didn't have much humor left. "Open seating. That's why I enjoy coming here, usually."

"Kate, are you okay? This has been one hell of a night for you. I am so grateful you didn't get hurt. This guy is crazy. I'm talking psychopath beyond belief. The people they believe he murdered...he terrorized them, then he hacked them to death. The only reason I'm mentioning this is I don't want you to hear it on the news or read about it in the papers."

I sat silently with Miss Joy on my lap and Mercy leaning against me. They were my comfort and support. I knew I was tired from the long ordeal and the mass of people, but I was still not jaded enough to have no feelings for the folks he had frightened and killed. I was also thanking God that He had given me enough courage and stamina to stay alive and keep my dogs safe.

I knew Gary was waiting for me to answer his questions. "I'm all right, just thoroughly confused about why these things happen to me. I mind my own business, don't interact with people, and yet, I am, always it seems, in the midst of some fracas. What is wrong with me?"

In what I assumed was an attempt to be comforting, Gary lifted his arm and placed it on my shoulders in a half hug. "It isn't you, Kate, it's the way the world is now. It has become extremely difficult to tell the good guys from the bad ones. You have to assume they're all bad until they prove otherwise."

I thought he might have some merit to his way of thinking. I also knew me well enough to know I would never adopt the same ideology. "When will this troop of folks get out of here? They have him...what more do they need? After they clear out, perhaps I can stay for a few more days and relax with the dogs."

Gary shook his head. "No, you won't have peace anytime soon, I'm sorry to tell you. The press will hound you to death. First, the local papers and news people, then the tabloids. They are all like sharks on a feeding frenzy. Imagine the headlines: Lone woman camper captures escaped crazed killer single handedly while he was in the midst of a national killing spree."

My mind hadn't even gone down that road. What a dummy. I needed to contact my kids and friends to let them know I was okay. Then the next thing would be to find a hiding place. I hated any kind of publicity, for anything. Gary had stated the obvious...this was going to get ugly. The recent mess on the island had been kept to a bare minimum due to the nature of the situation. This would be vastly different.

Dana arrived with the news I was needed back at the scene for more answers to the same questions. Thankfully, I'd had the presence of mind when I walked away with the dogs to lock the camper so they couldn't invade all of my space. I didn't want to return, nor did I wish to speak with anyone else. It seemed I didn't have a choice, because they had followed Dana and we were surrounded.

A man who appeared to be in charge introduced himself as Trooper Wilson. He stepped forward and told me he needed to complete a report requiring information from me.

I most always try to be as compliant as possible, but my patience had been bruised beyond repair. "Sir, I don't mean to seem rude or disrespectful. However, I have spoken with dozens of you folks and told all of you the same thing. I really believe if you take the time and listen to any one of them, you have all the information you need. I just want you to all leave, take him with you, and let me be here in peace. Is that too much to ask?"

I guess it was, because he looked like he was ready to have a full-blown stroke.

I felt Gary's arm tighten on my shoulder. Most likely not a good sign. He leaned forward and spoke quietly. "Trooper Wilson, this has been a horrific time for her, and, from my perspective, she is right in the fact she has related the facts to several of you. I think she deserves to be allowed some downtime."

Wilson fairly bristled with indignation, "Who in hell do you think you are to question me or my authority? What in hell are you even doing here?"

Dana stepped up to the trooper and very quietly said something to him. I couldn't hear any of the conversation, which was short and evidently, to the point. The trooper looked startled, took two steps backwards, then tipped his hat to Gary and marched away without another word.

Okay, case closed, I guessed. Although I wondered why and what Dana had said, I was politic and polite enough not to ask. Gary, the dogs and I continued to sit on the boulder in silence. I wasn't naive enough to think this mess was over, but I would take what I could get at the moment, enjoying it as long as possible.

Dana had wandered off, and I assumed he'd joined the group down by the camper. I wasn't concerned about the rig because I knew

I'd locked it. My personal space was mine, and I didn't intend for it to be invaded for any reason.

We decided it was time to return to reality and were walking toward the gathering, which had grown and spread like a fungus. It appeared as though the entire area was filled with men carrying guns and now, they had also added dogs to the fray.

Just as I was ready to question Gary about what was happening, Dana came into view. He had something on his mind, which you were instantly able to discern by his walk and body language. Gary stopped to wait for Dana to reach us. All Gary said was, "This isn't good, whatever it is."

Dana stopped directly in front of us and gave us the news. "You two are not going to like this, but better I tell you than someone else. He wasn't alone when he broke out of prison. The person he was with, if possible, was worse than him. They have brought in some dogs to see if they can track where they were. They don't want anyone to leave the area right now. That includes both of us and you, Kate. They have sealed off the roads and the woods are full of men and dogs."

I just wanted to get into the camper and sit in blessed silence. They certainly couldn't disallow me that minor privilege. As I walked toward the camper, I stopped short and checked my memory. Gary was watching me and didn't understand why I had stopped. I knew I had left the kayak tucked safely under the rear of the camper. It was no longer there. I nodded toward the camper. "Why would they need to use my inflatable kayak, with all of the equipment they brought with them?"

Dana overheard my question to Gary and, nodding to us, he ran off into the throng of men milling around. There was a surge of bodies headed for the lake. Either the good guys had borrowed it, or we now knew there had been a second person involved. We didn't know where it was, though. Not good news for me either way. I knew it was the death knell for my very expensive inflatable. One more loss.

We reached the camper, and within the minute it took me to unlock it, I was asked about fifty questions, none of them making much sense to me at that point. I answered none of them. My mind was too tired. If I said anything, it would sound like gibberish.

Gary stepped inside with me and Mercy; I still had Miss Joy in my arms. The space suddenly seemed very crowded. I was finding it difficult to breathe. I needed to sit and stay calm, or I was concerned I was going to faint. I'm not a person who gets woozy easily, but I do know my limits, and I was way beyond the point of no return.

Seventeen

Dana came and knocked on the door while calling Gary's name. When Gary opened the door, I heard Dana ask, "Gary, they want to know if I can use the small bird to check for the boat, or if I can spot him because I can fly lower and faster. Your call, Chief."

"I don't care if you use the bird…just be careful. Are you going to take a spotter with you?"

Dana's answer was a snappy salute. "Yes, Chief. Keep your radio open. I'll keep you posted about anything I see." With that, he slammed the door shut and yelled, "Lock it now."

I leaned back on the sofa against the small throw cushions I keep on it. The next thing I remember was waking up from what had been a very comfortable nap. Somehow, Gary had found the warm throw I carry with me and had put my feet up and tucked me in on the sofa. Miss Joy was sound asleep against my tummy, and Mercy had my feet warm at the bottom. I always said I would suck as a night fighter. I require my regular sleep. I found Gary sitting at the table, snoozing with his feet up on the seat opposite him. I surmised we were both too old for this lifestyle.

I saw there was still a large group of uniformed people outside, although they didn't seem to be as noisy as they had been previously.

It was time for me to get up, make a pot of coffee, and find something to eat. At the first movement I made, Gary was wide awake watching me. I kind of chuckled to myself, thinking how I must have looked while asleep. My mouth was most likely wide open and snoring, or at the very least, drooling, or worse. Oh well, that's life at it's very best. After I get away from here, I'll never see him again and something else will fill in the slot that memory briefly had taken up. Life is good at these things.

I made coffee and produced a couple of my homemade muffins, so we at least had something in our stomachs. You would have thought I had served him a gourmet delight instead of a plain old blueberry muffin. I wondered if the men outside had any coffee. My pot is a two-cup small coffee maker. I didn't think I would even have enough to satisfy a quarter of them. Better to leave well enough alone.

Gary's radio crackled and we could hear Dana loud and clear. "I spotted the kayak floating off a cove way down the lake, but no sign of him. I will get someone to bring it back to the campground for you, Kate. I'll stay out for a bit longer, then I need to refuel. I think Bangor will be my best bet for that. Are you guys doing okay, or should I come get you first?"

Gary looked at me with a questioning glance. I just shrugged. "We're fine...do what you think is best. We'll be here when you return. Dana, if you spot him, don't do any hot-dogging...let them do the capture. We really don't have a clue if he is alone or has others with him. I trust they cleared the other camping areas when this first began. Stay safe."

We drank our coffee in silence and a horrid thought occurred to me. "Gary, if I wanted to escape from this horde of people, I would have ambushed one of them, put on their uniform, and strutted around with the rest of them. There are so many people here from all different agencies, who would know? How does Dana know who the person flying with him is? In a state of emergency, most likely he didn't check his ID or his bona fides."

Gary looked at me like he couldn't believe I had voiced such a crazy scenario. Then I watched while the idea penetrated his mind.

I think we both had the same thought at the same time. How could we verify who was flying with Dana and not give anything away which would jeopardize his safety? Dana could very well be flying the prisoner around with him, and if he went to Bangor and refueled, the person could force him to go who knew where. Then what would happen to Dana? Lord, I hoped and prayed this was just one of my lunatic pipe-dream ideas.

Gary opened the channel on the radio and I held my breath. "Dana, before you go to refuel, would you swing back here? I'll give you the necessary paperwork required to file a flight plan and purchase the fuel. Please roger that."

Gary looked at me with a worried expression. "Dana will know something may be fishy because he *is* the person who would file any flight plan. Let's pray he calls me right back. Then we'll know it's legit."

We waited, and Gary kept glancing at his watch. The minutes ticked by slowly, but no return call. I don't know what his timeframe was, but when he reached it, he headed for the door with the radio still in his hand. I chose to stay behind in the camper with the dogs. This could be a terrible situation, made even more epic if what we envisioned was happening.

I could see Gary speaking with one of the men who seemed to be in some position of authority. There were a lot of hand and body gestures going on. Another man joined the group. He was the man to whom Dana had spoken when we were sitting on the boulder by the shore some hours ago. The whole attitude of the group changed immediately. The new man's name, I recalled, was Trooper Wilson. He had a radio in his hand and was very intent on the conversation he was conducting. I noticed Gary's shoulders sag as if in defeat. Had they put his idea off as ridiculous? Or worse case...believed it; and now had another critical problem to deal with. Gary was heading back to the camper. I would know shortly.

I knew the answer when I spotted Gary's face. His friend and comrade was in deep trouble. Gary reinforced my concern. "Wilson has no idea who is in the chopper with Dana, and he has asked for any visual sightings to be reported to him ASAP. So far, nothing." Gary had activated the search for the radio beacon installed for tracking. It appeared it was now a waiting game. I prayed whoever was with Dana had no clue how capable he truly was. I wondered at what point in the odyssey Dana would realize who he had with him. I was certain he had been armed when he left here. I would also venture, with his background, he had more than one weapon on his person.

"Gary, how far could he fly before he needs to stop for fueling? Do you know what the person with him is capable of? His background before prison? Any military? Can he fly the chopper?"

Gary shook his head. "They're getting me pertinent information now. He can't have too much range on the original fuel left, so they will have to refuel soon if they keep flying. I can't believe I didn't even have a passing thought about '*what if*', until you mentioned it. I think I need to quit and go hide on the island until my time expires. This is the second time it was your thoughts which spurred me to get into the right lane. How in hell do you think of these things and be so damn accurate? I need to partner with you, or I'm going to get myself and/or someone else killed, because I'm becoming mentally deficient. I must tell you, I'm damn frightened for Dana. I'm serious. He's the son I never had, and this time, I'm beyond terrified. I should have gone with him. Then this wouldn't have happened."

Trooper Wilson knocked on the camper door. I opened it and asked him to come in. Now, the camper was way overloaded with people and animals. His first words were not encouraging. "I really don't want to relay any of this information, but you asked me to get it, so here it is. The man in the bird was a military mercenary before he was arrested. He was for hire to anyone or country who wanted anything done. He can fly the equipment...he is ruthless beyond imagination, and during his time of incarceration he's become beyond psycho. I haven't had any sightings reported. I have the word out to anyplace they could refuel and have no feedback at all. I wished I had better news. I will keep you posted. We're searching the woods for whoever he got the uniform from. I don't expect those findings will be anything except grim."

Eighteen

As Trooper Wilson was going back outside, and just as the door was swinging shut, Gary's radio began to crackle. Wilson stopped mid-stride and came back into the camper. We were all holding our breath when a different voice came over the airway. "If you want this silly son-of-a-bitch alive, you'll call and authorize a refueling. If not, I'll fly over your site and drop his body into the parking lot. I need you to roger that now."

Gary was as calm as could be. "I need to speak with Dana before I do any authorizing of anything. Roger that."

I could not believe my ears. I had also witnessed both of these guys in action and had great faith they knew what they were up against, and how to handle it. My heart was pounding so hard I was sure they could hear it outside, if not on the radio.

The radio crackled and Dana's voice spoke slowly. "Chief, I'm a kilo short of destination touchdown. Need voice authorization for tank one and reserve two. Would like to use customary procedure for payment. Please confirm."

Trooper Wilson looked puzzled. "What in hell is he asking? Do you know?"

Gary nodded. "He has about thirty minutes left of flying time, and the nerd with him is at the controls. He also has a gun on Dana and, in the process, Dana has also lost his boot gun and knife. He is also in restraints. He wants us to know he may need to kill this man and, while in the process, crash the bird. This is not hopeful, but he is determined not to let him live, even if he dies in the performance of eliminating the imposter. The voice authorization he is requesting is for me to tell him I agree. He does not want this idiot to have fuel or a flight plan, under any circumstances."

Wilson was astonished. "What are you going to do?"

Gary was silent for a second. I knew he was praying. "I'll do what we always do. Pray first, then fight to the death, if necessary. That's who we are."

Gary keyed the radio. "Authorization will be granted. I am reluctant to include reserve two. The refueling will need to be performed only by you and will require a signature with the usual stamp. Please roger that."

We all waited for a response. Time passed slowly as we continued to wait. Still no response. I'm not patient, and neither was Wilson. He had been standing, then he sat briefly, only to stand again and begin to pace. In the camper, there is no pacing room, but he managed. When he sat again, it was in resignation. Only Gary remained calm. I didn't know how, but I could sure use a lesson from him. I was ready to jump out of my skin. Even the dogs were restless. Mercy had her anxious face on. Never a good sign.

The radio came to life without the usual crackling sound. It had Gary's rapt attention as he motioned us to silence. We could hear Dana's calm voice saying, "We need to set down and change places prior to getting to the fueling destination. This bird has special clearance for fueling and only Gary or I have the authorization for operating."

Another voice came over the airways. "That's bullshit. How damn stupid do you think I am? This is a private chopper without any restrictions. I've flown enough of these to know the difference."

Dana's reply, although still calm, had an edge, "Okay, smart-ass, did you check the ID numbers on the craft before you boarded? If you're so damn smart, you would've known what they stood for. If we land with you at the controls, it will be curtains for you and perhaps both of us because I don't have the paperwork necessary for identification or to authorize a fueling or a flight plan."

We waited for more or any continuing conversation for several long empty minutes before Dana was heard saying, "We're about fifteen minutes out from our destination. The places to set down and change seats are going to be far and few between. Your call."

"Just shut your fucking mouth, idiot. You don't seem to understand I'm the man in control of this situation. You're handcuffed and I have your weapons, plus mine, so what's wrong with that picture?" Then there came the worse maniacally weird laughter I had ever heard. The hair on the nape of my neck stood straight up and cold chills rippled throughout my entire body. This man was certifiably crazy.

Dana's reply was short and to the point. "Do what you want. I'm ready to die either way. Have at it."

We could hear the sound of the chopper, but no conversation until the prisoner spoke. "Okay, moron, you may be ready, but I'm not. I have important plans. I don't trust anything you've said. I'll set down, and we'll trade spaces, but you need to know I don't have any issue killing you if you screw with me. Once this thing is fueled, you're my ticket out. I don't give a shit if you're dead or alive until I get ready to kill you. Do you understand what I'm saying?"

Dana was still calm with his reply. "Oh yes, you're in charge, and as long as I kiss your sorry ass, I live, for now. If you're looking for a spot to stop, you need to make a decision within seconds, or you will be in a zone which prohibits any landings."

While we were listening intently, Gary could hear the change of sounds as they were making a descent. He had no idea where they were, but knew the bird was being tracked. It wasn't helpful because if anyone approached, he knew the nutcase would kill Dana. He had already voiced his concerns with the folks doing the tracking.

The stress was evident on his face and posture. Trooper Wilson looked like a statue. He hadn't moved, and I wasn't sure he was even breathing. I wasn't doing much better. I hate drama, especially when it's evil and playing out in real time in my life.

I could hear the rotors still revolving, but slowly. I guessed it might have landed. Dana yelled in pain, "Look, ass-hole, if you break my arms, I can't fly, and you only have about fifteen minutes, if that, left. Make up your mind what you want. I need my feet loose, also, stupid."

There were sounds of scuffling, then, "You do anything dumb it will be the last thing you'll ever do. You're such a loser, I don't know how anyone with enough dough to own this crate would let you even sit in it, let alone try to fly it. Where in hell did you get your instructions? From a correspondence course or the internet? You are what I think of as a real jerk loser. I bet you don't even know how to shoot that pop gun you carry. One in the boot. Did you see that on a crime show and it looked tough, so you decided to try it? What a piece of shit you are."

We could hear the motor revving and prayed Dana was at the controls. I knew from things I had heard between him and Gary that Dana could thread the eye of a needle with the equipment.

"Why are you following the river north? If we're going to the airport, I can see it is to the west. Are you trying to screw with me, idiot?"

Very calmly, Dana replied, "With the classification of this bird, you can only fly on certain patterns. I told you before...this isn't a private toy. I do know what I'm doing and messing with an idiot like you holds no value or reward for me. Remember Siam!"

I looked at Gary; he was smiling. Had I been right all along? Were these two both crazy? Dana was in a chopper with a killer and almost out of fuel, and taunting him while his partner was sitting at my table in the camper smiling. Even Trooper Wilson looked shocked. Seeing Wilson's expression reaffirmed to me that I was still somewhat sane.

The next transmission was a stream of obscenities. Some I had never heard before, a scream which sounding like a wounded animal, then a gunshot. Oh, dear God, what had happened? There were no more engine sounds. Had Dana been shot? Had the bird crashed? All was quiet. What should we be doing now? I feared Dana was dead. I was heartsick. I had liked him, even though I'd never understood him.

I needed to know. "Gary, what do you think has happened? What does his reference to Siam mean? Is there any way to get information? Should we be doing something?"

Gary stood slowly and shook his head as if to clear away the mental images he had been carrying. Finally, he spoke. "We wait. I think I know what happened, but without a visual, I can't determine the outcome. Siam is a weapon we had made and incorporated into the seat of the chopper when it was built. It is a flat, rectangular, very thin blade, and sharp as a razor. Make no mistake, the bird is dead. I just pray Dana survived. Until we get notified, we have nothing. Do you have any more coffee?"

I couldn't believe my ears! "Coffee? At a time like this, you want coffee?"

"Yes, please, would you make some?"

I got up and began to fix coffee. I knew, inevitably, I would never make another pot of coffee without remembering this moment. When it finished, I poured a cup for Gary and one for Wilson. There was about a half cup remaining, so I took it. We drank in silence with heavy hearts.

Nineteen

The sound of Gary's cell phone ringing jarred us out of our lethargy. Gary carefully answered, while we held our collective breaths. "Yes sir, this is he. I understand. Can I call you back in a few minutes? Okay, I'll do that."

When Gary turned to address us, I couldn't read his expression. "Trooper, I need a ride and an escort, please. I think we can go faster by car than to wait for the time it would take you to get your bird returned. What do you think? Dana flew the chopper into the river after he went under the bridge. The moron is dead. Dana is in the hospital with some serious injuries, the least of them being a gunshot to his shoulder. I need to go at once. Can you arrange for us to travel? I need enough space for Kate, the two dogs and myself and something with speediness."

Trooper Wilson was out the door as Gary called back whoever had called him. Ten minutes later, we were speeding out of the camp road and onto Route 9 in a flurry of dirt and dust. We had an escort with lots of noise and flashing blue lights. The trooper was driving our car. He could have a future at Daytona. Every intersection was blocked off by a cruiser. We never stopped until we were at the hospital. We were escorted to a room to await any word from the doctors when they finished their surgeries.

Wilson had called the hospital explaining the need for special preparations concerning extreme privacy for Dana, Gary, and me, along with space for the dogs. He also had the foresight to restrict any press.

The staff plied us with food and drinks for the wait. There was very little conversation. I knew for certain there were plenty of prayers being said.

At last, the doctor, or I should say doctors, arrived. I was not encouraged by their expressions. Gary didn't look like he was, either. I prayed the shock of all this would not give Gary a heart attack or a stroke.

The doctors were careful and respectful as they delivered their prognosis. The first one identified himself. "I'm Dr. Cane, a surgeon. I was responsible for tending the gunshot wound and repair of the surrounding damage to the shoulder. I have every confidence that injury will heal successfully. I also repaired what appeared to be knife wounds to his face and scalp. He may decide to have a plastic surgeon do some final tweaks to polish my unhandy work."

The older of the three men stepped forward. "My name is Ken Christopher. I'm an orthopedic surgeon. Dana has several severe fractures, mostly of the compound nature. I have screwed, wired, and glued him back together as best I could. He will need some followup surgery for more corrections, if he survives. I am sorry this is not a very positive prognosis on my part. He will also require long term care, with a great deal of specialized nursing and rest, if and when he can leave this facility. The one thing in his favor, if there is one to be found, is the fact he is young and appeared to be in excellent health prior to the accident. I did note several old scars and evidence of old injuries. Was he accident prone prior to this?"

I had been watching Gary's face closely and had it not been totally inappropriate, I think he would have laughed out loud. I silently thought, if only they knew.

The last man to speak identified himself as Dr. Chan. "I'm sorry to add more sadness to the conversation. However, Dana received some devastating injuries to his internal organs that required some extensive surgery to stop the bleeding. At this time, he is still under anesthesia and most likely will be for some period of time. He will then require a great deal of meds for pain management. He may not be able to speak with you for a while, as I have put him on a ventilator. He was, however, very specific in his last request. I promised I would relay his message to Gary. He said to tell him, and I quote, 'the bird was dead, but died proudly doing his duty.' He also told me after he caught his breath from the pain that 'the eggs were ok.' Does any of this make sense, or was he delusional?"

I looked at Gary. I couldn't understand the expression on his face because he looked relieved. How could that be? He had just received news that his best friend may not live, and he looked relieved. I will never understand men, least of all this one, or Dana, for that matter.

Gary stood and extended his hand to first Dr. Chan, then to the other two doctors. "Thank you for all of your medical expertise and taking the time to chat with us. Dana is very important to us. I especially want to thank you, Dr. Chan, for relaying his message to me. When can we see him? We realize he will not be conversant for a few days, and he will experience a great deal of pain. Sometimes just a visual will be of great value for those of us who are waiting."

Dr. Chan looked at the other two doctors and quietly spoke. "You can certainly see Dana, but I want to caution you he looks very compromised at the moment. I would request only one or two of you step into his room. As you would expect, he is in ICU with a private nurse. We will also keep you informed about any progress, or worsening of his condition. Please follow me."

Gary put his hand out, indicating he wanted me to come with him. I looked at the dogs and was about to refuse when Trooper Wilson nodded to me. "Kate, I'll stay with the dogs. You need to go with Gary. Take your time...we'll be fine right here."

I followed Gary and Dr. Chan down the corridor to the elevator, with Dr. Christopher and Dr. Cane bringing up the rear. When we stepped off the elevator, we walked a few feet to a large private room filled almost to capacity with electronic equipment. At first, I didn't even see the bed. When I did, I had to look away. I would never have recognized Dana amid the mass of bandages, tubes, and breathing devices. They had his arm and one leg in what looked like traction, although there were no casts on them. He was swathed in bandages around one shoulder and all around his chest. His face, what we could see of it, was a mass of stitches with the skin puffed and puckered all which ways. He looked like a jigsaw puzzle with gaps for missing pieces. I wondered how he was alive. I was just thanking God he was.

Gary did a much better job of not revealing his shock at his friend's condition. He walked to the side of the bed where Dana's somewhat good arm was and placed his hand in Dana's hand. Even the arm was wrapped in gauze in places where blood had seeped through.

I watched fascinated as Gary very gently squeezed the motionless hand twice. After a second or so, Dana's fingers slowly coiled around Gary's hand. I heard Dr. Chan's gasp of surprise from behind me. I turned and observed the faintest of smiles on his lips, and a look of pleasure in his eyes. He nodded to us and stepped outside the room.

I felt I'd just witnessed a very special moment in the lives of two people. I also felt like an intruder, so I quietly backed out of the room and stood in the corridor. Dr. Chan was speaking with the other doctors, telling them of the reaction. Now all three were nodding and grinning.

Gary stayed for another few minutes, then left the room. He came and stood next to me and spoke to the doctors as a group. "He'll make it. I've watched him survive worse under terrible circumstances. We'll be back later to check in on him. Thank all of you once again for the care you've given him."

We left the hospital with Trooper Wilson and headed back to the camping area to retrieve my rig. We were still several miles away from the camping area where I left it and I was shocked to see my camper parked alongside the road in a spot designed for truckers' use. When we pulled alongside, there was a man sitting in the driver's seat. Now what?

Trooper Wilson was quick to assure me it was fine. "I had one of my men move the rig so you would not have to deal with a bunch of press or gawkers. We just told them it was going to impound. End of interest. Gary, where are you parked? Can I give you transportation?"

Gary smiled. "My transportation was fished out of the river, what was left of it. They were kind enough to dispense with the corpse for me, and retrieve my paperwork from the bird. I'm fine with Kate, for the moment, and I really don't think she should be left alone right now. Thanks for the offer, though. If you need additional information to wrap this up, call my cell."

Twenty

We let the dogs do what dogs do, then boarded the camper. I wasn't sure where Gary wanted me to take him, but I was certain we would make a plan after we got buckled in. I did admit to myself I no longer felt in charge...of anything. How had my life gotten so sidetracked?

I guessed, even if I weren't in charge, I was the one who needed to make a plan. "Where would you like me to take you? Did you fly off the island? Do you have a vehicle on shore? How long do you think Dana will be in the hospital? How did you know what his response would be when you squeezed his hand?"

Gary laughed. "You are the queen of questions. I want you to take us to someplace where nobody knows where we are. We did fly off the island. Yes, I do have transportation on shore. Dana will be out in a very few days. I just wanted him to know I was there. He did, and now he will relax and get better. Do you have enough gas to drive to the shore?"

"Well yes, depending on which shore we're talking about. With you guys, it's hard to stay connected to one thought for more than a nano second. Where do you want to go?"

Another chuckle. "Are you familiar with a small town called Trescott?"

"As a matter of fact, I am. I sold some real estate there a very long time ago."

I started the motor and drove east. To where, I had no clue. I mentally asked myself if it really mattered. I was tired, but so riled up I couldn't even begin to unwind. Thankfully, driving always tends to calm my senses.

Once we arrived at the coast, Gary began giving me directions. I knew this area somewhat and I was shocked when we turned down the Crow's Neck Road. It was the same road I'd sold property on.

When we turned off the main road, we came to a locked gate. Gary got out, unlocked the padlock and motioned me through, then closed and re-locked. He directed me to drive down the heavily tree-lined road for a distance. He asked me to stop while he exited the camper. He walked to a tree, reached his arm up to the lower branches, then got back into his seat. He nodded for me to drive forward. I had no idea where we were going. I did know I couldn't turn the camper around on such a narrow lane, and backing out in the dark was out of my wheelhouse at the moment. We turned a sharp corner where I could see an area large enough to park several vehicles. Would wonders never cease?

As I swung into the parking spot, floodlights came on in every direction. They were so bright it was startling. Gary seemed unfazed. He spoke quietly. "What do you need to take out of the camper for the night?"

I thought for a moment and decided it would be easier for me to just stay in the camper with my dogs. I was ready to declare my intentions, when Gary shook his head and said, "No way you're going to stay out here. If it seems too difficult to grab a few things, I'll loan you one of my t-shirts for PJs."

The mental picture flashing through my mind spurred me to grab my camp bag and stuff a couple of things into it.

The lighting was so intense I couldn't see a dwelling anywhere. I followed Gary with the dogs at my side. Talk about blind faith...this was the epitome of it.

The camp was built in such a fashion it sat in the trees, being totally hidden behind the boughs. I couldn't determine if it was a log home or board and batten. It was small, but because it seemed so dark after the barrage of lights, I couldn't make any determination.

Gary opened a door and inside lights began to glow. I saw we were in a large open space with comfortable furniture and a fireplace. Off to the side was a small kitchen. There was a hallway with doors leading from it. I decided it was a larger building than I'd first thought. "Take whichever room you are most comfortable with. They both have a private bath."

Although I had the notion the cottage had been closed up for a period of time, the air in the room seemed fresh. There was a comfortable looking bed, two overstuffed chairs, a bureau and a tall chest. I could see an open door leading into a full bathroom and what I assumed was a door to a clothes closet. The floor was wooden, with a very soft oriental carpet under the bed and was large enough to leave a comfortable walking space all around. The dogs quickly found their spaces to claim. Miss Joy was curled into one of the chairs, and Mercy was on the carpet at the foot of the bed.

My primary interest was the bathroom. I felt dirty, knowing I'd been sweaty then covered with dust, along with the smell of fear which still clung to my clothing. I wondered if a good warm shower would calm and quiet me enough to at least relax a little. I felt like my body had been on screech for so long, perhaps it had forgotten how to let down. I found the bathroom fully outfitted with even a long, very soft terry robe hanging behind the door. I took advantage of every second of hot soapy water, then dried on thick nice-smelling terry towels. By the time I left the bathroom, my questions had all been answered. Yes, I could still unwind and relax, if only for the present. That truly is all we ever have, just this moment.

I had begun to turn down the bedding when Gary knocked softly on the door. "Kate, would you like some warm milk and a piece of toast before you turn in?"

The thought of anything to eat or drink hadn't penetrated my brain, but now with his suggestion my stomach rumbled. How fickle am I? "Thanks, Gary, that does sound good. I'll be right out."

We sat at the table in the nicely appointed small kitchen enjoying the light snack and quiet company. I think we had both shut off our minds to the horror of the past few hours and the aftermath. We were both old enough to know the scenario would return when we were up to dealing with it. For now, we were just two folks enjoying some peace and quiet.

I slept like a baby, waking to bright sunshine. Both dogs came to attention as soon as I opened my eyes. We greeted each other while I gathered the robe so I could take them out. I tried to be quiet and not disturb Gary. My worry was unfounded as he was sitting on the porch drinking coffee when I opened the door. I was startled, because he appeared relaxed and calm like any person enjoying their vacation at a peaceful seaside cottage.

I'd expected him to be anything except calm and composed. I began to wonder what his secret was. Whatever it was, I wanted some. The moment my feet hit the floor, I had begun to replay the previous day in my head. I always do the *what ifs*. Was Dana still alive? How would Gary feel today? Would I be hounded when I arrived home later today? On and on it would go until I finally could manage to shut it down to a dull roar.

When Gary spoke, he knocked me out of my shock. "Good morning, Kate. How did you sleep? Would you like some coffee? I'll cook us some breakfast when you're ready."

"Thank you. Coffee would be nice. I need to get the dogs their food, then I'll be right back. By the way, I slept like a baby. Nice bed."

When I returned to the porch, I found the mug of hot coffee Gary had placed there along with, of all things, a piece of Danish pastry. I wasn't even going to try to guess where he got it. The man was magic. I would just enjoy the treat and let it go.

In the daylight, I could see the shoreline. The cottage sat at an angle with a view across the small bay. There had been enough clearing of the lot to allow the view, but unless you knew where the building was, you would not spot it from the water, nor, I realized, from the air. Clever, and nicely done. I admire good work and proper planning.

The mug of coffee will have to go down in my memory as one of the best I'd tasted, and the pastry was delivered by an angel from Heaven. I was shocked to find I was also relaxed and enjoying the morning respite. Perhaps there was hope for me yet.

After a trip to the camper for clean clothing, I tried to engage Gary in a conversation about my heading home and transportation for him. Gary's response was predictable. "Kate, you can't be serious about going home yet. I'll bet there are at least a dozen reporters from local and national news stations camped out on your front door. My transportation is not an issue, as you will soon discover. I would really like it if you would go with me to see Dana today. Do you think you could do that for me?"

"I would like to make sure Dana is doing reasonably well before I leave. You do understand I have to go home at some point. I live there. It's the only place I have to go other than the camper. I have almost always felt safe and somewhat secure in my homes and campers. However, these last few weeks have almost destroyed any pretext of my security. I can't allow it to happen, or I'll be like the rest of the rabbits running from den to den while hiding out. I need to feel free so I can enjoy what time I have left in this life. I don't know what you and Dana share as a secret to remain so calm with all the conflict and craziness that has happened since I first met the two of you. It must be a learned response, and I need to find it also."

Gary's laughter filled the morning air. I wasn't sure if he was laughing at, or with me, but it was a welcomed sound. Happy to be amusing. At the very least, I was good for comic relief.

"Kate, there really isn't any secret. After you have been threatened and given up for dead so many times, there just isn't any 'fear factor' left in your system. Both Dana and I have been at the end of our lives too many times, and we've beaten the odds and survived. We are both aware, acutely so, I might add, that we have probably used up our quota of near misses. Thus, the reason we decided to come to Maine and retire. Our plan was to do some fishing because we both enjoy the water, and perhaps fly down to the islands for our winters and sit in the sun. Our plans seemed to go off the rails when an old friend of mine recommended that we check out the drug running along the coast. Because we were unknown to the natives, we would be in a good position to just 'observe.' We had begun day one when the murder on the island happened and we met you. Now, that is history. Then we were sitting on my island enjoying a beer and lamenting too much peace and quiet when you called me this time. Neither of us ever anticipated what has happened to either you or us."

I drank my coffee and tried to digest what Gary had shared. I shook my head, trying to clear out my feelings of guilt at causing all this mayhem for both of them. It didn't help. I still felt I had somehow cursed them. I knew Gary was scrutinizing my reaction. I was beyond trying to hide my dismay. Usually, I know how to fix most things I screw up, but this time I had no clue, and I'm certain it registered on my face. I never was a good bluffer. I suck at poker.

"Kate, you have to understand, none of this mess is of your doing. You have just had the misfortune of being in the wrong place at the wrong time. The other side of this situation would be to think about if someone else had been camping there. They would have been killed and nobody would have been the wiser, until the killers were long gone and on to murdering others. Those two would never have stopped until they were dead themselves. I don't even want to think about how many others you saved. Now the bright spot in all this is the fact that you knew Dana and me. We not only had the resources but were bored to distraction when you called, so you killed two birds with the one proverbial stone."

"Gary, in a rear view of what happened, I don't think that was a good analogy. Sorry, I know you want me to feel better and I appreciate your effort. The truth of the matter is clear. Dana is badly injured, you have lost an expensive piece of equipment, and I will probably never draw another breath without looking over both of my shoulders."

His smile told me he wasn't buying my version. "Dana will recover. He will always be a 'soldier' and he will be paid well for his part in getting rid of the vermin. As for the equipment, as you call it, it was insured and will be replaced. So, for us there was no harm and no foul. Now to your peace of mind, it is something you have to make your own decision about. If you want to be free to enjoy what you want and like…do it. If you want to spend the rest of your time hiding out like the 'rabbits' you mentioned, then do that. It's a choice only you can make."

I understood the truth in what he said. It was my decision and mine alone. I would deal with it. I had overcome horrific situations in my many years, although not as terrifying as the last couple days/ For certain, I would survive and be all right. I was instantly reassured, as Mercy laid her head in my lap and snuggled against my leg.

Twenty-one

It was time to move on. I looked at Gary and suggested we needed to get going if we were to check on Dana.

I showered and changed, getting ready to go to Bangor when I heard Gary go outside. He was walking into the woods behind the cottage. When he came back in, I needed to see if he wanted to use the camper to travel in.

I walked out on the porch and headed toward the camper to put stuff away when I heard a motor start. I stopped mid-stride. When I said a 'motor' start, it would be like comparing a piper cub airplane to a jumbo jet. Lord in Heaven, what a sound! The rumble from the motor would have made my son's teeth chatter in jig-time. Now he could and would appreciate this machine. When Gary drove around the corner of the cottage, I couldn't trust my vision. There was an old battered Downeast truck complete with fender rust. One thing was for sure, nobody would be taking a second look at the truck, no matter who was driving it. Unless you knew engines, you would never guess what it really was. And here I thought I was the only one who supplied comic relief. Wrong again.

When Gary stepped out of the truck, he was grinning from ear to ear. "I forgot to tell you we like funky-rides, too. What do you think? Does it pass muster for being understated?"

We loaded the dogs and rumbled to Bangor. I was correct in my assumption that nobody would ever guess who we were. Gary parked in the parking garage. I was concerned about leaving the dogs in the vehicle until Gary explained the security system on the truck, which he had tucked into a back corner where there were no others parked.

We walked into the hospital through a side door and were promptly met by a security guard. Without a word, and with just a nod of his head, he escorted us to a private elevator and we were whisked to the ICU floor. The guard motioned for us to wait while he went to the nurses' station. When he returned, we followed him to a different area than where we had seen Dana the night before. This was either good, or bad, I was unsure. When the guard opened the door, I was in awe. It was a large private room and, although he still looked like a train wreck, Dana was awake and not connected to a ventilator. He smiled when we came in.

Gary walked over to the side of the bed, nodding with a big smile. "Hi there, cowboy, how're you doing?"

Dana's smile stayed in place while he responded, "I'm doing well, as long as I don't sneeze. Then I'd worry something important would fall off. How are you two doing?"

"We're fine, driving the Downeast limo and hiding out in the pines. Are they taking good care of you? What do they think the biggest issue is, or haven't they gotten that far?"

My part in this visit was to observe and stay quiet. I stood and listened as they chatted as if a few hours ago the doctors hadn't been certain if Dana would survive the night. Talk about seeing a miracle. I was witnessing one right then, in real-time.

Gary's question regarding the cuts on Dana's face almost had me looking for a place to hide. "How did your face get so damaged? All the glass in the bird was synthetic."

Dana tried to appear nonchalant, without success. "The idiot was a cutter. He had bragged about how he had fileted some of the folks alive and was really getting off on it. I didn't respond to him, so he wanted to elicit some 'respect.' He decided he would carve me up a little. He'd searched me and taken all my weapons, but he failed to find our Siam we'd built into the seat. After a couple of swipes, I'd had enough of him and didn't give a damn, so I slid it out and gave him some of his own treatment. It got pretty hairy for a few seconds, then he shot me. I knew if I buried the bird and he lived, he would be free to continue his reign of terror. I sliced his neck and he was gone. It was too late to pull out of the descent so I ditched. Sorry Gary, I loved that bird."

"Not to worry...it was well insured and we'll have another shortly. I think we may need to go bigger and with more toys if we continue to associate with Madam Mayhem here."

They both enjoyed a good smirk over the reference to my personal penchant for disaster. I was so happy Dana was alive, I didn't care.

While we were still with Dana, a man came to interview him about the incident. He told us he was only allowed five minutes. It was evident from their greetings, both Dana and Gary knew him. I stood aside listening, confused about how three grown men could discuss such a terrible situation, not to mention how injured Dana was, as if it were an everyday occurrence. I almost concluded that, for them, perhaps it was.

When he completed his discussion, he turned to me and requested an audience with me regarding my role in the capture of the first prisoner. I looked at Gary. I didn't know this person, who he was, or what he wanted. My only wish in this mess was to remain anonymous, finish with our visit with Dana, go back to my camper and drive away. Gary knew what I was thinking and volunteered, "I'll come with you, Kate. Snead is an okay guy, but if he gets testy, I'll take care of you. Okay?"

I nodded and we walked down the hall to a private office where we could talk without disturbing Dana or the staff. Once we were seated, the man known as Snead began abruptly. "I understand from the reports, you, an older woman, alone at a remote campsite in the middle of the Maine woods, captured a first class, nationally known and hunted killer, single-handed. Is that your story as well?"

I was not only taken aback by his condescending attitude and brutish manner, I thought he was unprofessional, ignorant, and an idiot. I was as provoked by his dismissive rhetoric and biased opinions regarding age and gender as I was about his body language, which betrayed his belief that I was lying. I should have learned after all these years, when I am not just angry, but ripping mad, to keep my mouth shut. However, "Listen, you pompous moron, I don't give a damn what you think or believe. I have no intention of sitting here listening to anything else you have to say."

I'm not sure who began to roar first...the idiot or Gary. It became instantly obvious I was being played by this dude, whoever he was. I totally failed to see the humor in the situation. I stood and headed for the door. They could both go to hell for all I cared.

Gary was the first to speak just as my hand landed on the latch to open the door. "Kate, it's okay. Please stay and find out what this meeting is really all about. I've known him forever and he has always been this way. Come sit here next to me on the sofa. I told him on our way down to this room he had met his match. See what disbelief will do?"

I was steaming and had no desire to continue any dialogue with either of them at the moment. "You guys can sit here and entertain yourselves. I will have no role in any of your antics. I'm going to say goodbye to Dana and then I'll wait in the garage with the dogs."

I marched out of the room and back down the hall to Dana's room, with Gary hot on my heels. I knocked on the door and pushed it open enough to stick my head in. I could see he was struggling with something in his hand resembling a monitor of some sort. He looked up, smiled, and asked me to come in. I wasn't sure if my entry would disturb him and cause discomfort, but I stepped into the room. "Dana, I wanted to just say goodbye to you and tell you how sorry I am for what happened to you. I didn't expect this outcome when I called Gary. I will keep your recovery in my prayers. I will let you get some rest now."

"Kate, not so fast. None of my injuries are your fault. I was careless. I didn't check out who was getting into my bird. A total breakdown of procedure. I know better. Gary told me you were the person who figured out I might have the other escapee with me. Thank you for that. Don't let Snead turn you off. He loves to be large and in charge, even when he's way off base. He needs to get you to sign off on this case so they can pay you the reward money. It's a substantial amount. Hold your ground, take the money, and enjoy the fact you had the moxie to do what you did and survived. Don't worry about me. I'll recover. I do need to ask you a personal favor, please. Will you keep an eye on Gary until I get out of here? I plan on being out in a couple of days."

I must admit my anger had cooled while talking with Dana. "I need to disappear, not babysit. I'm eternally grateful to both you and Gary for several things. I'll honor your request."

"Kate, thank you. Knowing you'll do it is going to hasten my recovery and ability to escape from here. I'll chat with you later."

When I stepped out of his room, I prayed I had not made another mistake. I wanted him to recover, but I wasn't certain about care-taking Gary. I also had no idea of the time frame involved. Too many unknowns for me. I like structure and black and white definitions. This scenario offered me none of those. I headed for the elevator to return to the garage. When I got there, I found Gary and Snead. I became angry all over again.

Gary put his hand on my arm and spoke quietly. "Kate let's go to the coffee shop and straighten this mess out. Right now, I need your help and so does Dana. I can certainly help you with the red-tape and paperwork involved in resolving the payment of the reward due you. Please come with me. I promise I will muzzle our alleged friend."

Snead was standing close enough so he could hear everything we were saying. He looked apologetic, but I doubted he had any ability to express it. As long as he kept his tone and words civil, I would do as Gary requested. If he reverted to being the idiot I assumed him to be, I was out of there. Gary could deal with him by himself.

We sat at a table in a nook to one side of the coffee shop. Snead, without a word, produced a folder and a pen. He passed it across the table for me to read. It was an accurate account of what had happened during the capture. He reached over and lifted the first sheet so I could scan the other documents. I was astounded at what I was reading. The bounty on the person I'd captured was $500,000.00. I couldn't begin to process the amount. He then lifted the sheet to reveal another. This sheet stated I had assisted in the capture and death of the other inmate and was intitled to a payment of $250,000.00. I closed the folder and looked at Gary.

I had no words, and I wasn't certain if I were still breathing. I mentally made a note that it was probably a good thing we were still in the hospital. My mind had stopped processing anything. Gary knew I was in shock. He looked over, smiled, patted my hand, and said, "Kate, have a sip of your coffee. I fixed it just the way you like. Take a deep breath and relax...everything will be okay."

My world had been so crazy lately I wasn't able to figure out what 'okay' really was anymore, or if it still existed. I think secretly we all hope someday we'll win the lottery, even if we don't play. It will just magically happen. We daydream what we would do if we didn't have to spend every waking hour and lots of sleepless nights trying to just manage and provide the basics. I know I did in the past and still have flights of fancy about doing something philanthropic. I was sensible enough to know any meager amount I could supply would never fall into that category. I smiled and waited for this dream to end and I'd wake up in my modest house in my own bed.

Gary reached his hand over to touch my arm. I think he was trying to remind me I was still sitting in the hospital coffee shop with other folks around me. It worked, whatever his intention had been. I looked at him and nodded to let him know I had returned, somewhat. I needed to finish whatever needed to be done to dismiss Snead and get outside to fresh air and my dogs.

Snead moved the file and turned back to the first page of the documents it contained. He never spoke, just indicated with his finger where he wanted me to sign. He handed me the pen, I signed where he pointed, he slid the file into his brief case and left.

Gary offered his hand to help me rise from my chair, and we strolled outside and into the parking garage. I was surprised when we left the shop another security guard began walking almost lockstep with us to the truck. Again, without any conversation. Standing against the wall behind the truck was another guard. We got into the truck and, when Gary started the motor, both guards walked away. Why, I wondered, were we being so closely watched? I didn't care enough to ask Gary. I wanted to go home.

I had called my children and friends when all of this happened, so they knew I was fine and so were the animals. I had also called my next-door neighbors and asked if they would keep an eye on the house. When I called later to check, I was told there were news vans parked in my yard, and the police in our town had been there several times to move them off my property. So much for peace and harmony on the home front.

We drove back to the coast in almost total silence. My mind went from chaos to blank then back to riot status. When we arrived back at the cottage, I walked into my room with the dogs and fell sound asleep on top of the quilts.

Gary and I never discussed the reward monies. I think he felt it was better left alone until I processed it and wanted to share some thoughts...or maybe not.

Each day we repeated our trip to Bangor to see Dana. Some days we stayed a little longer, depending on how he felt. I thought his recovery was remarkable. Dana thought it was too slow, so he vacillated between being depressed and euphoric. On the fifth day, Dana told us he would be leaving the hospital the next day. He had made all of the arrangements for transportation for himself and the necessary equipment he would need to convalesce at home.

When we were in the truck leaving the hospital, I could tell Gary seemed worried. "What's the problem? Are you not excited for Dana to come home?"

"Kate, that's not the issue at all. I'm delighted he is well enough, and I'm sure we'll manage just fine. I hope he isn't doing it too soon. We have plenty of room, and I know he'll recover faster with us than at the hospital. He wouldn't share with me how he was coming and that concerns me. So far, we haven't had any intrusions onto the property, and I would like to keep it that way. It will all be okay, don't worry."

I wasn't concerned because I'd been working on my own mental plan which I hadn't shared with Gary. When Dana finally got home, my plan was simple: the dogs and I were leaving and going away with the camper. We would stay out of sight until there was no further interest in the news stories. Everybody, even reporters, get sick of any story after a fair amount of time elapsed.

Dana arrived at the cottage in the early afternoon in what seemed, at first glance, to be a large delivery truck. Two men assisted him into a wheelchair and carried him into the living room. They proceeded to unload several medical devices for what I assumed would be for his rehabilitation. I took the dogs and went to the camper while Gary helped the men rearrange the bedroom Gary had been using into a comfortable space for Dana's recovery.

When the truck was emptied and the equipment properly assembled, the men drove away. Shortly after their departure, Gary knocked on the camper door. When I called for him to come in, he answered, "I need a hand here. Please help."

I opened the door to find him standing there with a bottle of wine, two glasses, a munchie tray and dog treats. I did the only thing I could under the circumstances. I laughed, then took the goodies so he could come in.

"How is Dana settling in? How are you doing?"

"Dana is taking a well-deserved nap at the moment. I, on the other hand, am a damn wreck. So, needless to say, I brought some medicine and hope you'll share space with me so we can get well together."

"I can certainly assist you with the medication. While they were busy moving Dana's gear in, I moved our stuff back out here to the camper so you can use that bedroom. I think it will be a bit unsettled in your home for a while. You two seem to care-take each other well, so I'm not concerned. As soon as you get your timing and scheduling restructured, you will both relax."

"Kate, I'm concerned because I'm not hearing any participation on your side in this conversation. I don't want you to feel I want you to care for Dana or his medical or rehabilitation needs at all. I'm being honest and very selfish here. I need your company and mental strength for myself. I'm asking you to help me get through this. Your moral support, sense of humor, positive attitude, and the dogs are such a blessing to me, I can't adequately explain them. Now that I've made a total ass of myself and shown you my feet of clay, let's have some of the wine and snacks."

Wow, there was a download in spades. I had no immediate response ready, so I opened the wine and poured. I needed to digest the proffered information before making a reply of any sort. I'd learned a long time ago not to make snap decisions without a lot of consideration, prayer and thought. Too old to change now, and I didn't want to.

We were sitting at the table sipping wine and eating snacks while the dogs were curled up on the couch sleeping pleasantly. I knew from experience when you are caring for a person who was badly injured, during recovery there wouldn't be many of these breaks. This was just the beginning of a very long recovery period for both Dana and Gary.

While we were sitting there, my neighbor, John, called on my cell phone, nearly causing me to spill my glass of wine. Very few folks ever call my cell. The call was somewhat distressing. A courier had arrived at my house to deliver a registered and certified packet. When the courier knocked with no response, he noticed my neighbor walking toward him. The courier inquired as to when I was expected to return and John told him, in no uncertain terms, it was none of his business. The courier took umbrage with that answer and explained it was *government business* and he needed to deliver the package at once. If John didn't assist him, he could be arrested. He passed John a card informing him he would return the next day for instructions as to how to complete the delivery. John gave me the information on the man's card along with a telephone contact number. I assured him I was fine and would take care of the matter at once, and also, jail was not in his future. John and I had a chuckle over that bit of foolishness.

When I finished the call, I shared with Gary what had taken place to see if he could shed any light on what was going on. He took out his cell and made a call. "Snead, Gary here. I just got some disturbing news. A courier was at Kate's home trying to make a delivery and threatening her neighbor with jail if he didn't assist in telling him where she could be found. Is this your doing?"

I watched Gary's expressions go from his usual bland to rip-shit in a half a heartbeat. When he spoke, his anger came out full force. "You're an idiot of the first magnitude. I've been trying to keep her sheltered from the damn press, and you sent someone out looking for her. On top of that, he threatened her neighbor with jail. Who in hell do you think you are? What the hell is the matter with you? You get in touch with the moron you sent and contact me. It's evident you can't even do a simple task without restarting World War Three. I personally don't think you could find your own ass if you had both hands free. Never mind sputtering, just do as you're told and call me back at once."

I smiled. "I'm happy you were here. Good job of taking care of another one of my issues. You need me to get out of your hair so you can get on with your life and retirement."

Snead wasted no time in calling Gary back. Before we had finished our glasses of wine, Gary had a meeting set up to procure the documents. He assured me there would be no more such foolishness. Gary then called someone else and alerted them to the fact if he had any more issues, he would call in needed assistance. I guessed it was not going to be needed because when he ended the call he said, "Thank you, sir. I knew you would understand the delicate nature of the situation. No, I don't think witness protection will be required in this case. It seems the problem is with our own crew. Is there no one left with a thinking brain in that division?"

Whatever the answer was, it got a hearty laugh from Gary along with, "No sir, I retired, remember?" He closed his phone, took a sip of wine and said, "Kate, taken care of. There will be no more problems. Enjoy your wine. This is the best part of my day. I hope you've enjoyed it as well."

The next day Gary helped Dana to get bathed, fed, and settled into his chair. He admitted he was tired from the trip home and wanted nothing more than to sit and watch some junky television for a while. He seemed quite adept at getting about with the chair. My guess would have been it wasn't his first time using one.

Gary told him we had a meeting planned later in the morning with the courier or his replacement if they hadn't fired him after his blunder. We would only be gone for a matter of a couple of hours at most.

"You two get out of here. I don't need anything I can't manage on my own. I want you to get this business over and done with. I'll be right here when you return. Kate, are the keys in the camper? I don't want to be tempted beyond what I can resist."

"Dana, the rig is locked and I have the only set of keys in my pocket. Sorry, no joy riding for you today."

We laughed our way to the truck with the dogs and drove off. It was fun to see Dana joking again.

Gary and I met the courier in the craziest place you could ever imagine: a lobster pound down at the harbor in Lubec. When I asked Gary why there, he smiled. "I want some fresh lobster, so why not? You do eat lobster, don't you?"

"Gary, I was raised on an island in Casco Bay. Of course I eat lobster, and most anything else that comes from the ocean."

The man arrived as scheduled, and on the hood of what appeared to be an almost derelict old truck with rusty fenders and half eaten rusty running boards, I received a packet containing banking information for way too much money. Sometimes life is too funny. The man was very careful and respectful to both Gary and me. I asked Gary why. His answer was hilarious. "Wouldn't you be careful around a little old lady who just captured a nationally known killer single-handed? I would be, except I know you and nothing you could or would do will surprise me anymore."

I smiled, punched his arm and we went off to buy seafood like two tourists.

I locked the packet away in a small hidden safe I'd built into the camper. I needed to secure a safe-deposit box as soon as possible.

Dana was in good spirits when we returned, so we all sat out on the deck to enjoy some sun and a glass of wine. Other than the fact Dana was still wearing some bandages, hadn't lost all of the stitches, had braces, and was sitting in a wheelchair, we could have just been old friends on vacation. When the breeze off the bay began to cool the air, we opted for indoor seating.

I offered to help Gary fix dinner. I liked the small kitchen...it was utilitarian, clean, and well equipped. The meal was delicious and very appreciated by Dana, who was certain the hospital was using previously frozen tv dinners and/or dog food to feed patients.

Gary assisted Dana in getting ready and into bed. Then Gary and I watched television for a while. I took the dogs out for a short walk, then we turned in for the night in the camper. Nice to be in my own space. I slept like a baby with the dogs cuddled up around me. My last thought was, perhaps it was just possible maybe life would regain some normalcy. Hope springs eternal in the foolish human heart, especially mine.

The days seemed to develop a pattern by themselves. I would get up early, as usual, let the dogs out while I fixed my coffee, then feed them. When Gary was up and about, he would step out on the deck and either whistle or holler across the yard to offer coffee and breakfast. He cooked, fed, and helped Dana while I cleaned up the kitchen. I would take the dogs for a walk. Sometimes Gary joined us. In the afternoon, I would use one of the kayaks and explore the bay area. Things were comfortable and peaceful.

During one of our afternoon walks, Gary inquired about my love of the water. "I notice you enjoy paddling about in the tiny kayaks. Have you always enjoyed boats?"

Easy answer for me. "Always. When we were kids on the island, my brother and I would 'borrow' any punt the owner had left the oars in. The lobstermen all knew who had their boats. They didn't care, and we were respectful of their property. I've always wanted to learn to sail. I just never had the time or the funds at the appropriate time.

I would love to learn to sail a small one-masted craft with perhaps a centerboard so I could sail in and out of coves. Perhaps I will still get to do it. I'll put it on my 'bucket-list' with all the other things I've wanted to do. Although, to be honest, I have already done most everything sensible folks would want and then some. How about you? Do you still have things you want to try?"

"Oh yes, actually I have quite a few. I always wanted to travel like a tourist and visit small towns, see the Rockies, go to Canada, and perhaps take a trip to Alaska. I think I would enjoy being just an ordinary citizen. I like my boat, but seldom use it for sport. I'm not sure why not. I would like to just enjoy a friendship with someone. I don't even know if that's possible. I always loved dogs and animals but have never had one. Not even as a kid, because my dad was military and we moved around a lot. I kept saying 'someday,' but it never happened."

Twenty-two

I was replaying my recent conversation with Gary on my walk
to the shore late the next afternoon to enjoy a short paddle with the
kayak when I spotted a person hunched over and walking stealthily
along the shore next to the treeline. Too many things had occurred
lately not to pay attention, so I stopped and stepped behind a large
spruce tree. I was careful not to move as I watched. The person was
wearing what appeared to be a wetsuit. He had pulled off the helmet
part, but the face mask still hung around his neck and had been
turned backward over his shoulder. He was carrying a small rucksack.
Something seemed familiar about him. He stopped, bent over, and
extracted a pair of small field glasses. He placed them on a rock next
to him. During the next few seconds, he pulled out and assembled an
assault rifle. He was inserting a large clip into it when I turned and
began a hasty retreat. I was extremely careful to be quiet, hoping not
to draw attention to myself. I didn't have the luxury of Mercy with me.
I felt naked.

I landed on the deck and burst through the door just as Gary was
rising from his chair. I gasped out, "Gary, quick, man on the beach."

Gary didn't understand why I was so flustered. "Kate, people clam
there all the time."

I almost screamed, "They don't use assault rifles."

Dana heard me and wheeled to the window. "Gary, why isn't the alarm system on? Kate, where is Mercy?"

"I left her in the camper because I was going for a paddle. I'm going to get her and my gun." I sprinted out through the side door and ran to the camper. Mercy was in guard mode, so she sensed something was going on.

My cell began to vibrate. I yanked it out of my pocket; it was Gary. "Can you see anything? Keep the line open. There has been a breech in the security system, so visual is all we've got. Who do you think it is?"

"I don't see anything yet. He had a small pair of field glasses, and he was wearing what looked to me like a wetsuit. He had the helmet off with the face mask still around his neck but behind his head. He appeared to be young and in good shape. I'll keep Mercy here with me."

Gary cautioned, "Kate, don't do anything stupid. We've got you covered from here. Dana is armed and ready. I may sneak out and circle the wood-line, so don't shoot me. I'll keep my cell on. I'm wearing the earbud. Okay?"

My mind began to go into overdrive. I knew what I'd seen. I also knew the figure I'd seen was somehow familiar, in a bad way. Why couldn't I place him? I'd been watching the clock on the microwave and knew I'd only been back in the camper for less than five minutes. I had my revolver in my hand and extra bullets in my pants pocket. Mercy was standing on the seat of the dinette, looking toward the woods and the shore beyond. Her head snapped to the right so quickly I thought she was going to fall off the seat. She began her low growl. Every nerve in my body responded. I quickly relayed to Gary, "Whoever it is, Mercy is looking to the right of the camper and growling. Where are you?"

Quick reply, "Not there."

I walked lightly to the rear of the camper. I have windows on two sides in there. I watched for any movement. I was sweeping the woods with my eyes for anything out of the ordinary. Because it was late afternoon, the woods were all in shade and he had been wearing a black suit. Unless he moved and I caught the exact moment he did,

I would most likely not see him. I continued to watch. Maybe he had circled back. I did have all the windows in the camper open and there was a slight breeze. It would be unlikely I would hear him. A visual was the only chance I had.

Mercy was standing beside me and I was tempted to lift her up and let her stand on the counter. Her eyesight was better than mine. I had begun to bend over to lift her when a movement caught my eye. "Gary, can you see the big maple tree down the drive? I saw a movement there."

"You stay inside the camper and don't let Mercy out. Promise?"

I kept my eyes fixed on the last place I'd seen the movement. What I wanted to do was take Mercy and sneak up behind him. I was worried I would be too noisy and we would both get shot. I would stay there and watch, unless something changed drastically.

Another ten minutes of cat-and-mouse and nothing. I was getting antsy. Not a good feeling.

I heard a burst of fire from the assault rifle. Oh damn. Silence. About a ten second pause and another burst of shots still from the intruder's rifle. I was horrified. Was Gary shot? When I was about to fly out of the camper with Mercy, there was a single shot from a handgun. I didn't know if it was safe for me to take a breath or not. Gary's voice came over my phone. "This is done if he was alone. I want you to keep watching for others. I'm going to have Dana call this in, then I'll re-connect with you. Stay in the camper."

I did as Gary requested and placed Mercy back on the seat of the dinette. She understood what I wanted. I could tell by her stance. She was intent on the woods, and especially where the path was leading to the shore.

I heard traffic coming in on the drive. I could see Gary speaking with a man, then another vehicle arrived with more men, and the ambulance came. I began to shake. I sat on the sofa and realized I was most likely having a slight PTSD attack. There had been so much violence in the past few weeks, it was compounding. I had to get a grip.

Gary came to the door. "Are you okay? Do you want to go up to the house? I'll be done here shortly. If you need me now, I'll have them wait. What would you like?"

"Easy answer…to be normal again. Why does this keep repeating itself over and over? Did you get hurt?"

I heard a snicker, "No, thanks to you. I had the advantage of knowing he was here, and where he was located. The reason he looked familiar to you was because it was Mike, the man from the first episode. Somehow, he had either been released from jail or broke out and was looking for revenge on Dana and me. He's dead. Are you sure you're okay until I finish up with them?"

"Gary, I'm an adult. Of course, I'm okay. Do you think he was alone?"

"We don't know. Dana is researching as we speak. I'll be right back. Get some rest."

When Gary returned, he told me Mike had escaped from jail alone. When they searched his rucksack, they found a supply of explosives along with ammo clips for the assault rifle and an assortment of small tools, including wire cutters. We decided to adjourn our visit and move to the cabin where Dana was waiting.

As we entered, Dana called out, "Another disaster averted, thanks to our personal super-sleuth, Kate. You know, we have got to keep you with us, or we're going to get killed. You don't have a choice but to take care of us aging veterans. After all, it's the patriotic thing to do."

"Very funny Dana, the answer is still 'no.' I really did have a life. All I want to do is see if I can find it again. Seems like such a small task. However, it's been much harder to accomplish. You two must be sick of this foolishness, too, or as I suspected all along, you're both nuts. Whatever the story is, you're going to have to find that out on your own. Let's have a glass of wine with a snack and call it a day."

While I was sitting there, I began to realize some facts. When you finish a day with an invasion, a man hunt, a shooting resulting in a person being shot dead and yet, sitting there having a glass of wine like ordinary folks do, something was seriously wrong with our lives, or with us as individuals. Man, I could write a book of questions that would keep the psychological community busy for eons. Most likely I still wouldn't have my basic question answered: "Why me?"

I knew it would create a firestorm of sorts; however, I was determined to speak my mind. "I am seriously ready to go home. I want to realize some normalcy in my remaining time."

Both Dana and Gary began the usual round of protests and I turned a deaf ear to both of them. I wasn't trying to seem rude; I just had not finished saying what I intended to articulate.

I shook my head and continued on. "I like you both and am happy and fascinated you both have the stamina and drive to continue your lives this way. I would rather go home, return to my relatively mundane way of life and be able to die of old age in my own space. That may seem like a waste of time to you guys, but it is my preference, rather than be killed by some idiot or mercenary with a grudge against who knows what. I understand dead is dead, however it happens. I want to enjoy some modicum of contentment *before* it happens."

When the sun set and the coolness of the evening began to descend, we adjourned to the kitchen to make dinner. Some things never change.

Twenty-three

Later that night, as Miss Joy, Mercy and I were waiting for sleep to come, I made my decision. No matter the circumstances, tomorrow we were leaving for home. I knew it was going to create a round-robin of discussions; however, I was leaving.

In the early morning, I readied everything for travel before I walked to the house for the morning coffee and breakfast routine. As I had anticipated, the moment I told the guys I was leaving shortly, all hell broke loose. I listened for a few minutes without saying a word, then got up, gave them each a hug and a quick peck on their cheeks, walked with Miss Joy and Mercy to the camper and drove away.

The moment my wheels hit the tar on the road, a great sense of freedom came over me. I was going home! Whatever awaited me there, I could handle. My phone continued to ring, so I shut it off. From now on, my life would be mine. I didn't even let my mind wander to what my property would look like after the amount of time I'd been away.

I drove up my road and swung the camper across the end of my driveway and backed into my parking space as if I'd only been away for a short time. It felt good to be back. I unlocked my door and entered the garage where my truck was still parked, just as I'd left it. It seemed suddenly as if it had been years since I left. When I unlocked my door to enter into the kitchen, I felt somehow like I didn't belong there anymore. It was not the emotion I had anticipated. When I looked at Mercy and Miss Joy, they also looked confused. This was not good. I gave myself a mental shake and proceeded into the living room and my bedroom. Instead of feeling welcome, I felt out of place. I was certain it would pass, or at least, I hoped it would.

I tried to return to my routine of living, but I couldn't settle into it. I couldn't figure out what was hampering my progress. I shopped for groceries, cleaned house, did laundry, and mowed the lawn. The summer had waned, and fall was approaching quickly. I realized my flower gardens were beyond fixing, so I began pruning them back. No matter how I filled my day, I couldn't find any sense of contentment or belonging.

I had done the appropriate banking with the funds I'd received. I managed to make some gifts to folks and organizations I'd always supported in a minimal way as my previous funds had allowed. Some had been done anonymously. The feeling of enjoyment from this was my best reward.

I felt somehow I'd lost a major part of who I was as a person. However, I couldn't get a handle on why. I'd lived all of my life mostly alone and on my own; that hadn't changed. Something had. I needed to find out what, or why, so I could try to fix it. I hoped and intended, with my usual flare for optimism, to live a lot longer, as most folks do. I knew I wouldn't or couldn't succeed while in my present state of mind. With that thought in mind, I gathered the dogs for an afternoon walk on one of our trails. Walking was always therapeutic for me.

I always carry my cell phone, even though I'd managed somehow, it seemed, to distance myself from my few friends since I had returned home. Partly because I had no intention of discussing what had been happening in my life. Also, the fact they felt 'left out of the loop.' Although I had never been very social, I could somewhat understand their position. I didn't wish to recall it and it would have been almost impossible to explain. When it rang, I was slow to pull it out of my pocket to check who it was. I didn't recognize the number, so I just let it ring. There are always robo calls and I ignore them.

We finished our walk and returned to the house. I had a strange thought just before I pulled into the driveway, before I would have thought we were returning to our home, not 'the house.' When had that changed? Oh well, another unanswered question.

While I had been away, so many things had changed, or was I just seeing them differently? I needed some clarity but hadn't a clue, for the first time I could ever recall, where to find any answers. I knew one thing for certain: I wasn't going to just keep going along the same way I had been. I seriously believed in the power of prayer, and I had been praying about my situation faithfully. I knew from past experiences God would answer, in His time. Perhaps I was asking Him for the wrong thing.

The afternoon was over and it was time for my customary glass of wine with a munchie while watching the news. I gathered things together with our special 'cocktail bones' for the dogs and we sat down to watch whatever was happening, when my cell again rang with the same unknown number. This time I figured I would put a stop to these stupid calls, so I answered it. I was abrupt with my conversation, "Do not call this phone again." There...that should do it. I turned on the television, took a sip of wine and stuffed a cracker with cheese into my mouth. I felt better at once. I had done something positive and progressive. I smirked to myself.

Before the next sip of wine, the damn cell rang again with the same number. Now, I was angry...what was wrong with this nut? I snapped it on and, before I could say a word, I heard a man say, "Help! I need help now." I paused for a second but didn't recognize the voice. I was ready to hang up when he repeated the same message. Who was this? Only way to find out was to ask. "Who is this? And why are you calling me?"

I nearly dropped the phone when he replied. "Kate, it's me, Gary, I beg you, please don't hang up on me. I need your assistance badly."

Since I'd left the compound at Trescott, we had spoken a few times, but why the new unidentified phone number? My curiosity was piqued. "What's going on and why are you on a different phone. Is Dana all right?"

As usual, I got a chuckle, and what I had come to know as a pat answer. "You still ask the most questions of anyone I ever met. Dana is doing fine. I dropped my phone overboard, so I had to use an old one I keep for emergencies until I replace it. When I do, I'll keep my old number. That's the reason I haven't had my number transferred to this one. How are you doing, are the dogs doing okay? Can I get you to assist me with a project? One I know nothing about and you are well versed in?"

I smiled. "Who's asking all the questions now? What's the problem? Yes, the dogs and I are doing fine. If we weren't, I wouldn't tell you anyhow."

Somehow the back and forth of words had brightened my day incredibly.

Might as well ask the question and see what he needed. "What is the issue you need assistance with? I can't imagine anything you would need that I would have any expertise in."

Another chuckle. "Oh yes, you have me beat hands down on this one. I wondered if you would be willing to meet me in Bangor, and direct me in buying a recreational vehicle. I really want and need your assistance and insights on this. Will you assist me with doing it?"

Of all the things I could have conjured up in my mind, it would never have even been close to this. "Sure, I'd be happy to help. What brought this phase on? How much have you researched it? Do you have any clue of what options you would like? What class of vehicle are you thinking about?"

I got the usual chuckle, along with a laugh. "See why I need your help? I didn't understand half of what you were asking. Can you do it this week? By the way, when you come, I want you to bring the dogs, please."

The dogs? I was puzzled. "I can do it tomorrow if you can. If that's too soon, tell me where and when you want to meet. My time is pretty open."

Gary and I agreed to meet in the late morning at a dealer I knew. I had purchased some rigs there over the years. It would be a fun distraction to my morbid attitude and perhaps push me into a positive mental space. I still couldn't grasp the concept of Gary wanting a motor home.

I also had no idea this trip would make a major change in my life.

Twenty-four

We met at the dealer's lot as planned. I tried to get a sense of what Gary intended to do with the rig without seeming to be nosy. I was having no success. We needed to have an honest conversation or we would be there forever without a resolution. The salesman was of no help because he had no direction from either of us. I suggested we go sit someplace and have coffee or lunch and discuss what was needed, then come back.

As much time as I'd spent with Gary and Dana, I really knew very little about either of them. On the other side of the coin, they really knew nothing about who, or what, I was. I guess when it's a draw, someone needed to at least give a little, if we were going to make this venture work.

I'm always bold enough to begin, so I did. "Gary, what on earth is going on? What brought about the sudden urge to buy a traveling rig? You have a boat, plane, and I assume another chopper, along with several cars and trucks. Why this, and why now? Why isn't Dana doing this with you?"

Gary looked a little startled at all the questions. "All right, I'll come clean. If the FBI ever needs an interrogator, I'll send them to you. First, I'm going to tell you this is all your fault, in a good way.

"Dana is presently on his own adventure. He is fine and recovering well. He met a lovely young lady while doing his rehab, and they have become very close. I think he will be engaged shortly. They're going to live, for now, at the house in Trescott. The accident changed his mindset, along with your telling us we were a bunch of 'late-bloomers' in the growing up and bad boy category.

"Remember the day you told us why you were going home? Dana and I talked about that conversation a lot after you left. At first, it was kind of in humor, then we began to do some assessing of our own personal situations and directing a focused look into our own lives. We soon realized neither of us had done but a few of the things we really once wanted to do. We were both getting older, and, as you already know, I have a lot more years on me than Dana.

"You and I have never spoken much about our private lives, but you said some things and asked me questions which caused me to take an honest look at myself. With the few years I hope I have left, other than Dana I have no friends or family, and neither does he. I know a lot of people, but they are not, nor will they ever be, friends. I want to see if I can, in fact, be just a citizen, like other folks. I've wanted for years to travel and see parts of the country I'd never seen. I love animals, but have never been able to have a dog, cat, horse, or even a bird. I'm not certain I ever had a 'second childhood.' I was too busy being a wild man thinking I was invincible.

"To tell the truth, I think my feet of clay have finally come into full view. Did my confession repulse you?"

To say I was stunned would have been the understatement of the century. "No, I admire the fact you are being honest with yourself and me. You've lived this crazy life forever, while on the other hand, I just fell into it for a few weeks. It changed me in ways I don't understand. I can't seem to return to my 'old life' that I'd lived for most of my life. At first, I thought it was the aftereffects of PTSD or some such thing. It isn't. I still don't know what it is. I just know I need to change something.

"How do you think the rig will help you meet your goals?"

Gary smiled, looked a little scared, then blurted out his thoughts. "I want to buy a rig for the two of us and the dogs to travel in. Don't get angry with me. Please! I have terrible personal skills. Another fact I discovered and don't enjoy. I can shoot someone, but don't know how to have a polite conversation that isn't focused on a problem. Let me try this again, if I may. You understand camping and how the thing works. I know nothing about it. I also am asking if you would take me out and show me how to be civil, social, and to enjoy some traveling. I'm not looking for us to be anything except friends. I don't think I'm doing a very good job of this. I do better when you ask me questions than I do on my own." He ended with a smile and a laugh.

I just sat back and tried to digest the conversation without my usual response, which would have been to bolt to the nearest exit. I have encountered some strange and weird situations in my life. This one was at the top of the 'what on earth are you asking' list. I needed more than a cup of coffee to figure this out.

Gary was watching me with a hawk-eyed expression. I could see he also thought I was going to bolt. He was very calm when he asked, "Can we go back to the dealer and just look? I know I've sprung this on you and you need time to process the idea. It will be fun to just prowl through the lot and imagine, even if we don't do anything else today."

We returned to the lot, explained to the salesman we wanted to wander and look on our own. We spent a couple of hours looking, while joking about all the problems we could encounter with such a hair-brained situation. Because we had both relaxed, it was a fun and funny time with a lot of joking about the 'what ifs.'

However, at the end of our search, we had both settled on a class C unit with solar, a full kitchen with oven, a large bathroom and comfortable separate sleeping arrangements for two adults. I was surprised at how much the rigs had changed since I last looked for one. I always bought a used rig and mine was in the ancient category. When we took it for a test drive, Gary insisted I drive. Not a problem for me, because I love to drive and am more comfortable as a driver rather than a passenger. Since I'd never driven a brand new one, I decided to just enjoy the thrill of the journey, even if it was only a short one.

When we returned to the lot, I was ready to call it a day and head for home. The day had been a great distraction from what had been going on in my life. I was thinking perhaps with some of the funds I'd received, I might consider trading my rig and hit the road for a long trip. The idea had merit. I thanked Gary for a fun day and was ready to hop into my truck and drive away when he laid his hand on my arm and said, "We aren't done here yet. I need you to come inside with me while we wrap this up."

I'm certain my expression mirrored what my mind was thinking. I was confused. I was certain we had looked at everything he needed to see. What else did he need? Well, I'd gone this far…I could invest a few minutes more. I told him I would walk the dogs for a few minutes, then I'd join him in the office. He smiled and walked into the building.

When I found him sitting in the salesmen's office with a very satisfied grin pasted on his face, I began to be concerned.

The salesman also looked very satisfied. He rose from his chair, rounding his desk with his hand extended to me while saying, "I am certain you will totally enjoy this rig. It's one of our best sellers."

I stood there like a dummy. What was he talking about? I realized he was passing me an envelope of manuals and papers. I will give him credit; he was fast, because before I could utter a sound, he'd left the office, closing the door firmly on his way out.

I looked at Gary, who resembled the cat with the canary feathers sticking out of his mouth. "What have you done? Why is he giving me paperwork? Does he think I'm your file clerk?"

"Congratulations, madam, you now are the owner of a brand-new Class C motorhome with lots of extras. Even if you decide you can't tolerate me, I know you'll enjoy this rig. I cannot, and do not want this registered or recorded in my name. I want to become, and stay, invisible. It's yours, bought and paid for. I'll give you funds to pay for the registration, insurance, and to furnish it, but I don't want my name on any of it. The camper will be serviced and ready next week. What you do with it from there is up to you. I hope you will at least consider letting me enjoy it with you and the dogs. Let me walk you to your truck before you kill me in a public place."

I must have appeared to onlookers to be having a full-blown stroke. I know my jaw dropped; I was certain my eyes were bugging out of my skull, and no sound was emitting from my open mouth.

True to his word, Gary took my arm and led me to my truck. When he motioned for the keys to unlock it, I came to life. I shook my head 'no' so violently I nearly fell over in the parking lot. The movement activated my brain, along with my mouth. "Gary, I have no intention of taking this rig. I'm happy to assist you in getting it set up and showing you how to use a campground. I'll bring my rig and park next to you during the tutorial, but as far as traveling with you, it is never going to happen in a million years. I'm a loner, period."

There we stood at a total impasse, Gary looking as if he had lost his last friend in the world, and me with nothing but grim determination showing on my face and extending to my rigid posture.

Gary hung his head and looked like a dejected two-year old. "Please just think about this before you toss the whole idea. I think we could have some fun enjoying the road and each other. None of my intentions are nefarious, honest. I really want to explore parts of this country I've never seen. I know you love to travel and by your own admission, no longer feel comfortable doing it solo. We enjoy each other's company, so what's the issue? I also love the dogs. I promise you I will keep you and the dogs safe. Please just think about it. I would ask you to have dinner with me, but I have the feeling you would rather stab me with a steak knife than eat with me at the moment."

I had to snicker to myself. He was correct about the steak knife part of the speech. I needed lots of alone time to even begin to process any minute part of this afternoon. I unlocked the truck and slid behind the wheel. "We need to talk after I process some of this conversation."

I drove away from the lot and headed down the interstate. I was smart enough to not even engage in any dialog with myself at the moment. It was hard not to think about it, as the envelope with the new rig's papers were sitting on my dash in front of me.

When I arrived at my house, I played outside with the dogs, then as part of my usual routine, I poured a glass of wine and provided the dogs with their usual treats for the time of day. I would not engage my mind on any level with regard to the events of the afternoon. I am great at denial. With that thought in mind, I watched the news, ate a quick pick-up dinner and retired. I was searching for peace and calm as I began my reading of my Bible and the associated lesson books I use each night.

I'm a very prayerful person with incredible faith that God not only hears, but answers our requests, even from someone as rough around the edges as I am. He does this in His time and His way. I asked for His assistance to give me direction for this new situation.

When I opened my daily lesson I read, then re-read. I'm going to share what was written there. "Be willing to go out on a limb with Me. If that is where I am leading you, it is the safest place to be. Your desire to live a risk-free life is a form of unbelief. Your own longing to live close to Me is at odds with your attempts to minimize risk. You are approaching a crossroad in your journey. In order to follow Me wholeheartedly, you must relinquish your tendency to play it safe." To say I was stunned would be an unadulterated understatement.

I feel, in my personal opinion, I played it safely. Truthfully, I admit, over the course of my years I'd found myself in more 'situations' than the average person. I'm not a daring nor a careless person. I just believe today is the only day you have, so why waste it. To be honest, the recent scrapes were somewhat unnerving, considering my age. I began to realize I was not always going to be able to just walk away. I really didn't want to give up on doing the things I enjoyed; however, I knew doing them alone, even with Mercy to assist, I was on borrowed time. The world had changed and so had I. I understood the world's changing, not so much mine.

To say it was not a restless night would have been a bald-faced lie. I still didn't have a clear picture how, or if, this lunatic scheme would work. The fact I was still mulling it over made me realize I was obviously considering it.

When Gary called the next day to check on my progress with the idea, I was at least rational while asking what I considered intelligent questions. I was doing what I considered a good job until he told me they would be delivering the camper to me the next day. I knew it was either buy or fly time. I couldn't procrastinate any longer.

I was up early and moved my own camper down to my lower drive so they could park the new one in the appropriate place. Somewhere in my mind, I knew I was going to try this out.

The camper arrived as promised and placed where I directed the driver to park it. I waited until they left after my careful inspection of the unit to really investigate the interior. My mind was in a turmoil; certainly. I liked the rig. I had selected it. Could I really share space with anyone? A space this constricted? I knew myself well enough to know the longer I puzzled, the more unsure I would be.

I walked into the house and sat in my office for a few moments, then made my decision. At this age, what did I have to lose? I wasn't through wandering, and the last episode had shaken me to the core. What would be the harm of sharing a trip with someone else? I had spent enough time with Gary to pretty much understand him. He was not a gruff person...he was polite; he had never given me any cause for personal concern. I guess my bottom line was I didn't want to travel alone with the way the crazy world was at the moment. I also knew the general situation was not going to improve any time soon. I was certain if it was not working out, I could leave and come home.

I called Gary and told him of my decision and inquired when he would like to try a maiden voyage. His answer was spot-on Gary. He wanted me to give him a call and five minutes to pack his ditty bag. I think he was ready to hit the road.

I moved gear out of my own camper, then headed out to stock the cupboards for a short trip. I had done this so many times in my life, it was second nature. My mind kept going back to the 'what have I got to lose' question. Basically, nothing.

Our first trip was to a familiar spot for me on the ocean. I was surprised and pleased how quickly we blended the chores together. By the second evening, as we were sitting out by the fire enjoying our wine, it felt like we had always been doing this. The dogs were happy and comfortable, as witnessed by their places. Miss Joy was curled up on Gary's lap sound asleep and Mercy was curled at my feet. My life had taken a new turn. I was going to enjoy it for as long as it lasted. You can never ask for more than that. Truly, the moment we have is all we have...ever. Life is short. Enjoy it.

Meet H. Wakefield

H. Wakefield has resided in the wonderful, scenic and diverse state of Maine for all of her 83 years. She shares her semi-rural home with Miss Joy, an aging but energetic, miniature Australian Shepherd. Miss Joy is her constant companion for hiking, kayaking, RVing, and long drives in their classic truck. Her hobbies are varied, including writing, painting, home renovations, birding, fishing and most any activity outdoors. She has owned, or been owned, by many different animals throughout her lifetime, including horses, dogs and cats. To put it briefly, she has enjoyed and continues to enjoy her life to the fullest.

Her first book, *The Boat,* was very well received, surprising her as a first-time writer. Her second book, *Man in the Woods,* was anticipated by her readers and also greatly enjoyed. To her surprise and delight, the books have been enjoyed by readers of all ages and backgrounds. They love her style of storytelling. One reader remarked that, "it took me away from my hum-drum situation and transported me to another dimension. Please keep writing." And so, she has.

Other Works From The Pen Of H. Wakefield

The Boat - Eileen moved to a remote area on the Maine coast, buying a long-abandoned cottage seeking a sanctuary. However, her answer to a phone call said it all: "Oh by the way, I've been shot at, killed a man, my home has been invaded by lawmen, then my home was blown up along with my Jeep. But not to worry, I'm fine and so are the dogs."

Man in the Woods - What I thought would be a great real estate investment nearly got me killed, several times. In the midst of the mayhem, on a short jaunt from Maine to Virginia with my motor home, I tangled with a semi-truck while being stalked by a truly crazy woman.

Letter to Our Readers

Enjoy this book?

You can make a difference

As an independent publisher, Wings ePress, Inc. does not have the financial clout of the large New York Publishers. We can't afford large magazine spreads or subway posters to tell people about our quality books.

But, we do have something much more effective and powerful than ads. We have a large base of loyal readers.

Honest Reviews help bring the attention of new readers to our books.

If you enjoyed this book, we would appreciate it if you would spend a few minutes posting a review on the site where you purchased this book or on the Wings ePress, Inc. webpages at:

https://wingsepress.com/

Thank You

Visit Our Website

For The Full Inventory
Of Quality Books:

Wings ePress.Inc
https://wingsepress.com/

Quality trade paperbacks and downloads
in multiple formats,
in genres ranging from light romantic comedy
to general fiction and horror.
Wings has something for every reader's taste.
Visit the website, then bookmark it.
We add new titles each month!

Wings ePress Inc.
3000 N. Rock Road
Newton, KS 67114